PRAISE FOR SHA
&
ALL YOU C

"McKenzie's prose strikes like a sledge-hammer to the belly and a baseball bat to the crotch. He writes one-hundred-percent BALLS TO THE WALL, and I'm certain his name will soon rank high on the short list of effective extreme-horror authors."
—Edward Lee, Stoker Award winning author of *Brain Cheese Buffet*, *The Bighead*, and *Header*

"Unflinching and uncompromising, tough and talented, Shane McKenzie stands at the forefront of the next generation of horror writers."
—Bentley Little, Stoker Award winning author of *The Summoning*, *The Store*, and *The Haunted*

"Edward Lee fans are going to dig All You Can Eat! My advice? Devour this in one sitting, before it eats you!"
—J. F. Gonzalez, Author of *Survivor*, *Back From the Dead*, and the co-author of the *Clickers* series.

"Shane McKenzie has a wonderful grasp of the dark and terrible. He truly understands what terrifies us and his love for the horrific comes through in every ghastly sentence he composes."
—Wrath James White, author of *His Pain*, *Population Zero*, and *Like Porno for Psychos*

"Shane McKenzie's prose churns with horror, strangeness, fun, and unease. He's an exciting new voice in the horror genre."
—Nate Southard, author of *Just Like Hell*

"Shane McKenzie has the kind of imagination that should require a license to operate. He is one to watch."
—Ray Garton, author of *Live Girls*, *Crucifax Autumn*, and *Sex and Violence in Hollywood*

deadite press

DEADITE PRESS
205 NE BRYANT
PORTLAND, OR 97211
www.DEADITEPRESS.com

AN ERASERHEAD PRESS COMPANY
www.ERASERHEADPRESS.com

ISBN: 1-62105-031-9

Printed in the USA.

ALL YOU CAN EAT

SHANE McKENZIE

deadite
press

This book was my first actual sale, and a lot of people helped me get to this point. First of all, I want to thank Jeff, Rose, Carlton, and everyone at Eraserhead for taking a chance on me and welcoming me into the Deadite family. A big thank you to Nate Southard who read through the first draft of this and didn't tell me to go fuck myself afterward. Thank you to Kevin Wallis, AJ Brown, and Lee Thompson for all the help early on. Thanks to Jessy Marie Roberts for letting me run with my ideas. Thank you to RJ and Boyd at Cutting Block for helping me better understand what it takes to get an editor's attention. Thank you to all the fine folks at the Zoetrope offices. And of course, thank you Melinda, my wife, for all the support through everything. You read this book and are still married to me, so in my eyes, you're a bad ass motherfucker.

CHAINSAW DISCO BLOODBATH: THE SHANE MCKENZIE STORY BY NATE SOUTHARD

The house looked normal enough. Hell, the house looked downright quaint. A brick two-story in suburbia, a few cars in the driveway. Normally, I get nervous the first time I enter somebody's home, but the exterior of this place was so calm and quiet that I felt perfectly at ease.

"*Naaaaaaaaaate!*"

Shane greeted me with a shout that shook my bones. He was wearing a luchador mask, tuxedo shirt with the sleeves torn off, and suspenders. It was a one in the afternoon on a weekday.

Fine, that last part is a lie. It was a Saturday, and I was there for a Halloween party. Still, the rest of it was true, and the dichotomy between the loud, slightly crazy Shane and his quaint, cozy home is a fun little metaphor for the man and his writing.

That's the thing, ya dig? You don't see Shane McKenzie coming.

I mean that. I sure as hell didn't see him coming. A couple years back, I received a few emails from Shane, who also lives in the Austin area. It's always good to meet a writer living in your hometown, so we exchanged a few emails back and forth. At the time, Shane was largely working as an editor, writing fiction when he wasn't busy putting together anthologies. Right away, I found myself impressed with the guy's drive. He was reaching out and snagging stories from amazing writers like Bentley Little, Joe R. Lansdale, and Jack Ketchum. These are writers who still intimidate me, so his gumption left me a little slack-jawed.

When I finally met Shane all face-to-face like, I was surprised by how quiet and cool he was. Shane talks to you in the laidback, friendly way that eventually takes control of everybody who lives in Austin. He's fast with a handshake, but that's about it. Everything else he delivers with an easy cool that makes you expect to see smoke curling around him. I'd tell you his voice pours out of him like coffee and honey or something like that, but I hang out with Shane all the time, and he doesn't need to know about my man-crush.

But I could go on all day about the strange and surprising little quirks that make Shane McKenzie the hombre he is. I could tell you how he's Scottish and Korean, and how that somehow makes him look Mexican. I could tell you how an ecstatic, enthusiastic Shane sounds calmer than a bored Shane. And sure, you could say I just did. I guess I'd have to tell you to shut up and stop being a jerky jerkface so I can finish my damn story.

Rude . . .

Anyways, so at the 2011 World Horror Convention, Shane told me about this idea he had for a bizarre zombie novel where the cannibalism would be caused by a strange form of gluttony. Immediately, I thought it was a fun idea. He asked if I'd be willing to read it, and I said I would. When the manuscript hit my inbox, I opened it right away and started reading.

I didn't see it coming.

Man, it didn't matter how laidback and cool Shane was as a person. It didn't matter that he was this everyday husband and father from the suburbs. The story he'd sent me was *insane*. Somehow, this guy I thought I knew had gone from acting like Bruce Wayne to being The Joker. Everything he writes is marinated in this chaotic, maniacal sense of fun. You might think you're sane, but listening to Shane talk story ideas for an hour will make you question every facet of reality. I'm not even sure the word horror accurately describes what Shane McKenzie does. And bizarro doesn't fit either.

Chainsaw Disco Bloodbath. That's the stuff Shane McKenzie writes. Yeah, that's it. Chainsaw Disco Bloodbath, baby. Spread that on your toast and smoke it.

Well, now it's your turn to read this wonderfully strange

story about obese zombies. I think you're gonna dig it. Shit, I know you are. Unless you don't like fun, jerky jerkface. You think there's something wrong with fun? What the hell's wrong with you?

Seriously, I need to wrap up this intro so Shane can get to his story. We're wasting time. Soup's on, and everybody has a spoon. You don't wanna miss dinner, do ya?

Now, meet Shane McKenzie. Say hello and enjoy yourself. He's the nicest psycho you'll ever meet.

—Nate Southard

HUNGRY

The man breathed through his mouth, labored and wet. An empty plate lay on the table in front of him, a brown stain where the food had been. Dribbles of grease striped his chin. He reached across the table and plucked the rectangle of beef from his wife's plate.

"Jesus, Tom." The fork dropped from her hand and clattered to the table. She squinted as her husband stuffed the meat past his teeth, chewed it with an open mouth. Masticated bits dropped from his lips and landed on his plate—he leaned over and licked them up.

"I'm...hungry." He spoke around a mouthful of beef, stared at her with vacant eyes, and burped out a dank and meaty odor.

The woman covered her nostrils with her forefinger. Her mouth salivated from the scent, as if preparing for vomit. "What's gotten into you?"

"I'm hungry. I want...buffet." He slammed his fist, chubby and hairy, on the table with the last word.

The woman scooted her chair back and stood. She sighed, ran her hand through her hair, walked into the kitchen. "I made us a healthy meal. Spent hours on it, and this is how you act?"

He jerked to his feet, knocking his chair over. His stomach bumped the table and the legs screeched as they scooted across the floor. "...*hungry*..."

"Tom, look at you," she said. "Things are getting out of hand...your weight. I saw the credit card bill."

He stopped, the abrupt halt jiggling his chins. His head slowly turned toward his wife and his brow furrowed like a slab of bacon, mouth hanging open as his breathing rattled and his tongue moved in and out just past his lower lip. The

13

purple circles around his eyes were deep as bowls.

"It's not healthy, Tom. I love you. I only want what's best. Going to that place every day? For a month? It has to stop."

He stepped toward her. She matched it with a step backward, desperate to keep distance between them.

"I'm hungry. My stomach…it hurts. I *need* it." He licked his lips.

"We can do this together. I'll cook your favorites." She kept taking blind steps deeper into the kitchen while he pursued. Her back hit the wall and she forced a smile. "I only want to help you."

He turned toward the stove where another helping of beef lay in a pan, reached out and wrapped his fist around it. A low moan oozed from his throat as he shoved it into his mouth and his teeth mashed into it; he swallowed big chunks whole.

"Tom?"

He slid his feet across the tile until his gut pinned her to the wall.

She whimpered and turned her head as his stench, spoiled food and sweat, engulfed her.

He reached out with broth-dripping fingers and took hold of her arm. "I need food. I need the buffet…*it hurts.*"

"You're *hurting* me."

He leaned his head over her and sniffed, eyes fluttering and nostrils stretching wide.

She tried to pull her arm free, but his thick digits held tight, dimpled her skin with the grease-soaked fingertips. As he smelled her, a wet rattle emanated from his throat; he groaned and shuddered.

"My stomach…it needs it. The buffet. *Meat…*"

He dropped his head and bit into her arm.

His teeth grinded back and forth into her flesh, shoving through to the bone. Blood gurgled around his mouth, and she screamed, her eyes widening as the burn in her arm raged up her shoulder. Her knees went weak, but she was held up by Tom's grip.

14

He jerked his head to the side, the chunk of meat still attached to her arm by a strip of skin. When it tore free, it sounded like paper ripping. The woman shuddered and whimpered as her husband chewed the red and yellow mouthful, smacking his lips, pulverizing the meat with every crunch of his teeth. Blood coated his chin like a beard.

She wept, took gasping breaths, tried to gain her footing but slipped on her blood that continued to pump from the gaping hole. "Tom, no…"

"*Mmmm…*" He swallowed.

She found strength and hammered at his chest with her other hand, her wedding ring gleaming and stained red. Tears and mucus streamed and slid down her face as her arm throbbed, and her heart ached.

She slipped out of his grip and cracked her tailbone on the kitchen floor.

His frame blocked out the fluorescent light above them. A string of red drool oozed from his lip and puddled in her lap as he descended.

Her legs kicked, sliding in the blood, her tennis shoes squeaking.

She was awake while he devoured her. His weight trapped her as he took bites from the fleshy parts of her body, his breath hot and fetid.

"*Mmmm…hungry…*"

A NEW PLACE

Juan tumbled into the bodies next to him as the panel truck lurched to a stop. In the darkness, he couldn't tell who sat with him or even how many others there were. He could only hear their whimpers, their rapid breathing.

The trip was long and hard; he had no idea how long they'd been traveling. The air in the cramped space was thick and musty: body odor, urine, and excrement mixed with the sting of vomit, a result of those suffering from motion sickness.

But the truck had stopped. Juan didn't know what that meant. *Are we finally here?* he thought. He hoped so, and could only be thankful that his wife and daughter weren't with him. His mind flooded with worry at the thought of them going through the same long journey in the future. *If* he could raise the money.

What seemed like hours ago, he heard the unmistakable sounds of rape, somewhere on the further end of the truck toward the front: grunting and guttural moans over the gasps and squeaking of an unwilling female. Juan started to do something about it, started to climb blindly through the darkness to help whoever this poor girl was, but he couldn't risk it, had to put his family first, so he stayed put, stayed seated. And nobody else moved to stop it either.

"¿Donde estamos?" a woman's voice chirped from somewhere to Juan's right.

A chorus of murmurs and weeping ensued. Juan wrapped his arms over his knees and pulled them to his chest.

The truck rocked and a door slammed.

The murmuring raised in volume and intensity. Prayers began flowing from unseen lips, pulling tears from Juan's eyes as he thought about his wife and daughter, what he left behind.

The back door swung open and harsh sunlight engulfed them. Juan squinted, held out a hand to shield his eyes from the burn. He turned his head and saw the others; all packed tightly like sardines in a tin can. Their feet and pants were caked with shit-piss-puke stew. Brown faces stared out, some trying to dash toward the opening, toward the new beginning they had all hoped for.

A red-faced man in a straw hat frowned at them like a sunburned toad. A toothpick shifted from left to right and he snorted then swallowed. One eye clamped shut as he studied the group. He shoved an older man in the chest who'd managed to push to the opening. "Get yer ass back there. Not yer stop, Jose."

Juan peeked past the man and into the brightness of the day behind him. They were parked in a narrow alleyway, the walls decorated with graffiti and questionable stains. Trash cans lined the alley and stray cats paused in mid-stride to watch the commotion.

The man swatted Juan's knee, sending it clanking into his other one. "You, Jose. Get up and get out."

Juan looked back at the others for a moment, but their stares of envy and longing were too much. He nodded toward them—none nodded back—and jumped out of the truck, stretched his aching body. The man sized him up with his one eye, the other still squinting, and spat a wad of yellow mucus just between Juan's feet.

"Where is he? Yer cousin?" The man slammed the truck door shut, knocking a woman backward before concealing her and the others back into darkness. He pulled a pistol from his waistline, held it at his side. "He better show, Jose."

Juan's eyes widened to perfect circles. "Manuel...he come. Please." Juan searched the alley, but there were only two places to look: left or right. And Manuel wasn't in either. His throat went bone-dry and the spit he tried to swallow got stuck there and turned into a lump. The taste of acid stung his mouth as his stomach churned. "Please..."

"You got about another two minutes. I got more deliveries to make and don't have time for this bullshit." Another wad of phlegm, this one splatted on the toe of Juan's tattered tennis shoe. The mucus absorbed into the dried filth that was already there.

Juan wondered if he could make a run for it. Even with this shoes no better than papier-mâché, he figured he could outrun this flabby, wrinkled pig in front of him.

"You even think about runnin' and my pistol will fart a mess of hot lead into yer brown ass." He pointed the gun at Juan's chest.

"I'm here!"

Juan and the man turned to their left. Manuel jogged toward them from around the corner, panting, his breaths rattling.

"Keep yer voice down, Pablo. Shit." The pistol was lowered and placed back behind the man's belt where a roll of pink fat nearly concealed it.

Manuel trotted until he stood between them, leaned over with his hands on his knees and gasped for air. Juan could see that the American life had padded his cousin: gut hanging over his belt and puffy cheeks glistening with sweat.

"Where's my fuckin' money? I ain't got time for this."

Manuel pulled a wad of cash from his pocket, handed it to the man. He eyed the money for a moment, then nodded. "It's all there."

The man thumbed through the bills, spat on the concrete, walked back to the driver's door. The truck rocked, then took off.

Juan waved the exhaust out of his face, choked and snorted. He could only hope the rest of the people would get where they'd hoped they would and that whoever was waiting for them showed. He could tell that pistol had spat death into more than a few Mexicans, and that the man's finger had no trouble with squeezing down on a trigger.

"Cousin. Good to see you," Manuel said in Spanish, still struggling to catch his breath. Rings of sweat darkened his shirt at his chest and armpits.

"That was a nightmare. A fucking nightmare. I can't let my family ride with that man." Juan took deep breaths, and even with the slight tinge of garbage, the air was delicious.

"A girl was raped. Right next to me."

"Look, man. You're here, right? I kept my promise, didn't I?" He clapped a hand on Juan's shoulder. "You hungry?"

A smile cracked under Juan's black mustache and he nodded.

"We can get cheeseburgers for a dollar. And pretty fucking good, too." Manuel laughed as he led Juan out of the alley. "Not as good as your food, but it will do for now."

"I see the Americans have been feeding you well," Juan said and slapped his cousin in the stomach.

"Fuck you, man. Eating healthy is too expensive. And I just gave most of my money to that fucking coyote."

Juan put his hands up in mock surrender but couldn't wipe the smile from his face. As bad as the trip was, and though he wondered more than once if he would survive it, he was damn happy to see Manuel. His happiness was coated with a hint of regret for leaving his wife and baby girl back in Mexico, but they were safe with his mother-in-law, regardless if she was a bitter hag or not.

Manuel wrinkled his nose and then really looked Juan over. "Maybe we should get to my apartment first, get you cleaned up. You smell like you took a bath in shit."

"Not too far from the truth."

Juan took in his surroundings and felt his stomach plunge into his shoes; he'd never felt so lost in his life. He pulled the photo of his family from his pocket and stared at it for a moment, taking in their smiles, their captured happiness, and he could only hope they missed him too.

A FRESH START

Juan scrubbed the moisture from his head with a scratchy towel that stank of mildew, but he was thankful for the shower. His skin tingled and had already begun drying out from the hot, hard water and cheap bar soap. A scaly white film coated his hands and arms.

Manuel sat on his sofa and dug into a Chinese take-out carton with a plastic fork. He licked a few grains of rice from the fork prongs, eyes concentrating on the bottom of the carton, then looked up at Juan and smiled. "Better?"

Juan frowned. "Where did you meet that bastard anyway?"

"The coyote?"

Juan nodded, took a seat beside his cousin.

"He was waiting at the border at the same spot he picked you up, in that same truck. I showed him my money and he let me in. Sent so many others on their way, no matter how much they begged."

"And you trusted him? I thought I was going to die."

"It's not like we have much of a choice, cousin. I paid him, he brought me here. Same with you. Same with your family one day." He looked back into the carton, sighed.

"I don't think I can let my family ride in that truck with that son of a bitch. Did you see he pulled a gun on me?"

Manuel tossed the carton to the floor amongst the rest of the filth in the efficiency. He wrapped an arm around Juan, pulled him a bit closer. "Let me explain something to you. Out here, we are cockroaches. That's how they see us. A dead illegal Mexican? Nobody gives a shit. Get used to it, cousin."

"Then why come here? You promised me work, a better life." Juan twisted the fabric of the oversized jeans Manuel had leant him.

20

"You can have it. I already got you a job. It's not much, but let me tell you. It's better than selling gum on the street in Mexico. And the women out here taste like strawberries." Juan gritted his teeth. "What kind of job?" Not that it mattered. Juan would have taken anything. Since he was forced to close his taco stand back home, he'd been out of work. He had to swallow his pride and move in with his mother-in-law, who liked him as much as she liked cancer in her tits. So when he got Manuel's letter, explaining how he'd made it across and was living a good life, he jumped at the opportunity, promised his wife he would send for her and their daughter, bring them across to start over. He followed Manuel's instructions exactly, and there he sat in the crummy apartment on a squeaky, soft-as-steel-wool couch.

"You'll be working at the restaurant. With me."

"As a cook? You know I love cooking, but I can't cook that Chinese shit."

"No, cousin. Bus boy. You pick up the dishes, clean off the tables, sweep the floors, that kind of thing."

Juan's lip twitched and his mustache nearly made him sneeze. His eyebrow rose and he rubbed his clammy hands together.

"Look, it's the best I could do. You're lucky Mr. Chan agreed to take you in at all. The little fucker is mean. But it's work."

Juan nodded and sighed. Manuel was right, it did beat standing on the street selling gum to tourists. And it sure as hell beat lying to his wife, telling her he'd found a job, then picking a corner and rattling a coffee can for loose change. The Americans sure loved tossing coins to the local bums, like feeding the squirrels or something. They always had that goofy smirk when they did it, like it gave them a sense of well-being to toss a black nickel to a dirty Mexican.

Juan took a long look at the apartment. No bigger than a small bedroom. The couch, Juan assumed, was Manuel's bed. The floor was a mixture of empty food packaging, beer cans, and dark carpet stains. Manuel leaned over and picked up the carton he'd just tossed away a moment ago. He peered

21

into it and was disappointed all over again.

"I thought you said the food at the Chinese restaurant was terrible." He'd mentioned it in the letter. How rats wouldn't even eat the stuff.

Manuel crushed the carton and growled slightly. "It was. Could barely stand to smell it, let alone cook it. But Mr. Chan changed the recipe about a month ago." He wiped a coating of drool from his lower lip. "Noticed it smelled better and the customers seemed to like it. Now we can't keep the motherfuckers out. So I gave it a try."

"And?"

"It's...delicious. I can't stop thinking about it," he said. "But it's my day off today. Tomorrow, when we get off of work, I'll take some, bring it home for us."

"I start tomorrow?" Juan didn't like the feral look on his cousin's face, the way he seemed lost when he spoke about the food.

Manuel shook his head as if shaking away the cobwebs. "That's right, cousin. No reason to wait around."

Juan had never tried any Chinese food, and he wasn't very excited about it. If he had the ingredients, he'd whip up some tacos al pastor that would make Manuel shit in his Chinese carton. He longed to cook again. He was at peace with sizzling meat and vegetables under him, seasoning sprinkling from his fingertips. It had been far too long.

"So, now that you got the shit off your ass, how about those cheeseburgers?"

Juan's stomach gurgled and twisted. "Whatever you say."

ALONE WITH A
BOTTLE OF TEQUILA

Lola filled her fifth shot of Cuervo and tossed it back. It stung the back of her throat and she moaned and bared her teeth, fluttered her eyelids. She leaned back in her couch, her feet propped on an unopened box marked *Stuff* in black marker. The pounding in her head subsided as the liquor swam into her brain.

Goddamnit.

She eyed the joint she'd confiscated from the group of teenagers earlier that day. Jennings, her so-called superior officer and partner, did nothing. He sat in the car stuffing a sub sandwich down his throat like a seasoned porn star. The fat fuck didn't even notice or give a shit that they'd caught the little bastards red-handed. Told her to handle it, said it was her chance to shine—like busting some shit-for-brains teenagers would earn her any respect at the station. So Lola pocketed the joint, told the little fuckers to get a move on.

Of all the officers she could have been paired with. Why Jennings?

Every time she got in that fucking car, she couldn't get her father out of her mind. His grotesque, bulging body, his stink.

Lola plucked the joint from the table and jammed it between her lips. She lit it, inhaled deeply, sunk into the couch like an ember on a marshmallow. The sound of Jennings smacking as he chewed the cured meat and bread, slathered and oozing with mayonnaise still slapped around in her head. Her stomach turned and she took another long draw from the joint and held it in.

She heard her father calling her name from the other room, and she poured another shot of tequila to drown the ghost away. The voice turned to Jennings commenting on her figure, the endless innuendos. Her mind brought back images of her father lying naked in his bed, his bedroom door wide open...always wide open, stroking himself while drinking gallons of chocolate milk, eating tubs of peanut butter, the screams and shouts of porno movie after porno movie, flickering colors bouncing off his sweaty body. The bed sores crying tears of pus, giving off that stink that floated into her nostrils and refused to leave, even after all these years. At his funeral, she could still smell them, tattooed to the inside of her nose.

She coughed and choked as she exhaled, elbows braced on her knees. A string of drool drooped from her lip. The one picture she had of her mother, lined in its golden frame, stared at her from the coffee table, one of the only things she unpacked besides her dishes. Such a beautiful woman. Lola could just see the white jagged edge to the right of her mother's face, where her father's face used to be before she tore it out. Back when they took that picture, before Lola was born, he was actually a handsome man. He looked happy too, as far as Lola could tell from the photo. But she didn't know that man. She only knew the whale covered in wounds that refused to heal, gaping holes where scabs tried to grow but a jagged cuticle refused to allow them. The man that couldn't fit through his own bedroom door, not that he would have left the room even if he could.

She winced when the heat hit her fingertips. The joint had burned down turn to ashes while she glared at her mother, so she put it out, grabbed her box of cigarettes, knocked one loose. Instead of pouring another shot, she wrapped her shaking fingers around the Cuervo bottle, slid her lips around the spout, tilted her head back. The liquor poured directly into her stomach, and she nearly emptied the bottle before slamming it back down on the carpet. Her stomach threatened to reject it, to throw it back out from where it came, but she mashed her lips together and took deep breaths through her nose until the feeling subsided. She burped, long and guttural, then lit her cigarette.

The clock told her that there was still too much fucking

day left. She was too drunk and high to do anything but sit there and drink more. But she allowed herself these little binges, every few months or so, when the weight of everything threatened to smear her across the concrete. Tomorrow, it was back to work, back to normalcy. In the morning, she would have her daily five mile jog, then her hour of yoga, then a modest breakfast.

Keeping herself physically perfect was the only passion left, turning herself into a machine of lean muscle and rage. She made most male cops jealous, and they showed it with lewd comments and cat calls. But she wouldn't let them break her down, would measure dick sizes with any one of them.

Her father's voice called from the other room again, but she clenched her teeth and squeezed her eyes shut until they stopped. She would never go back to that house again. When she inherited it, it only pissed her off more, and as far as she was concerned, it could sit there and rot. A place for transients to shit, do drugs, and fuck. *Good for them*, she thought. The house was a prison for her fears and nightmares. A bloated, inflamed boil oozing pus and oil.

The cigarette smoke awakened the tequila in her belly, and she tried to hold it down, tried to persuade it to relax, but it wouldn't listen. She jumped to her feet, tripped over herself, fell face-first to the carpet. The room was a merry-go-round then. Warm bile exploded from her throat and puddled to the carpet, coating her teeth and lips. Then more came.

The smell... Daddy's calling her. She heard him clear as day this time, no question. Labored breathing. Wet noises like someone eating a lollipop.

Lola. Daddy's waiting for you.

"No. S-stop..."

More vomit, choking her, oozing from her nostrils, bringing water to her eyes. She tried to stand again, fell back to her hands and knees, crawled down the hallway, toward the bathroom. Warm chunky liquid squashed beneath her hands, between her fingers, under her nails. It soaked into the knees of her sweatpants.

My sweet baby girl. Daddy's hungry.

"F-fuck you..."

When she was nearly to the bathroom, she turned her head and peered down the dark hallway. She couldn't help but picture the flickering colors of a television flashing against the mound-over-mound of hairy, glistening flesh piled on the sagging bed.

She collapsed to her stomach and wept, cried so hard that each sob was like a punch to the stomach. Her breaths came in rapid rhythm, a wail between each one. She couldn't lift her head from the carpet, so she dragged it forward, pushing with her knees, the carpet fibers burning her face.

But she allowed herself these binges...every few months. To get her head straight...to face all of he pain, the memories.

In the morning, she would release her feelings on the streets. On the men that felt they ran shit, felt they could treat women like sex toys.

And she would do everything in her power not to puke all over her partner the second she laid eyes on the fat fuck.

FIRST DAY

The line stretched out the door. Round bodies shifted and bounced as they waited for their turn, watching the people within the restaurant eating. The house was packed; the cooks could barely keep up with how fast these people were eating. Puffy hands groped for eggrolls, fried wontons, crispy chicken wings. Thick fingers gripped serving spoons and piled on the General Tso's chicken, the pork lo mein, the beef and broccoli, all covered with thick brown sauce. Noodles dangled from the edge of plates.

Those within the restaurant sat at circular tables, none speaking, their language that of smacking, swallowing, and heavy breathing. Gargantuan men and women, sitting in small red chairs with their legs spread wide so they could fit, sipping soda between forkfuls of slop. Silverware scraped against teeth, chair legs screeched against the floor as the eaters stood to pile more food onto their plates.

Juan slid a damp towel over the tabletop, stacking used plates in his bus cart. The people hadn't been happy about being asked to leave, but with the line at the door, Mr. Chan placed a time limit. And the little spit-fire Chinaman didn't hold back. When the family of hogs tried to refuse, he laid into them, threatening to blacklist them, kick them out for good. That got the chubby bastards moving.

Juan didn't have a chance to introduce himself to his new boss before Mr. Chan started barking orders. Just another brown face to assign chores to. Juan could sense the little yellow bastard could barely tell the difference between him and the other illegal workers he'd hired. Manuel had warned him, but Juan couldn't imagine it would be that obvious. But he shut his mouth and got to work.

It wasn't long before the restaurant was buzzing and

people were stacking their plates and stuffing their bellies. Juan had never seen so much jiggling before.

Before he could finish wiping down the table, another family placed their coats and purses on the chairs and speed-walked toward the buffet. Their bodies swayed under their too-tight clothes.

Juan ran his forearm over his face and sighed. As he looked around the restaurant, he was overcome with a feeling of helplessness. A stranger in an unknown land. A lone turd floating in a sea of fat. The Americans were huge. Not like the ones he'd seen at home, all smiles while they bought cheap liquor and medication and whores.

He pulled the photo from his pocket, then lifted his pants back to his waist. Manuel didn't have an extra belt, and the worn-out jeans barely fit, the knees missing, only two belt loops left. The gray Dallas Cowboys t-shirt, some Goodwill hand-me-down that Manuel also had given him, was stiff and scraped against his skin. As he stared at the faces of his wife and daughter, he could have run right out of that restaurant and straight for the border.

"What you doing?" The sharp, high-pitched voice stabbed his eardrum like a poison-tipped needle. "Tables need cleaning. No time for break."

Mr. Chan ripped the photo from Juan's hand and squinted until his eyes looked completely shut.

"Lo siento...uh...sorry. I clean." Juan's eyes darted from Mr. Chan's tight scowl to the photo in his yellow claw. The Chinaman's face seemed to soften for a moment, just a fraction, then contorted back to a sneer. He tossed the picture to the table and walked back toward the line of awaiting diners. Juan snatched the photo back up, gave it one more look, fought back the tears, slid it gently into his pocket.

He pushed his cart, now crashing full with dishes, across the floor and toward the kitchen, passing countless blubbery bodies; the air vibrated with labored breaths. It smelled saucy and salty everywhere.

As the cart shoved through the double doors, he nearly ran over one of the cooks carrying a silver dish full of brown meat. Spirals of odiferous steam danced off it and were breathed in by the awaiting pigs. Tongues slithered over lips, eyes widened. The cook was nearly eaten alive as he set the dish at the buffet, then hurried back to the kitchen.

As Juan shoved his way in, the noise assaulting his ears went from the chaotic grumbling of the dining area to the sizzling of cooking meat and rapid Spanish shouting.

Paradise Buffet: a Chinese restaurant. Every cook Mexican, every one of them undocumented. Cheap, hard workers. Juan understood the concept, and wouldn't be one to complain since the money was all he cared about. The faster he made money, the quicker he could pay back Manuel. Once he did that, he'd be with his family again. He imagined they could get their own place, in a nicer part of town. Juan could learn better English, get a better job. And the best part of all, they would be as far away from that wrinkled cunt of a mother-in-law as possible. So he'd keep his mouth shut, nod happily, and do his fucking job.

"What's up, cousin? You having fun yet?" Manuel said as he dumped raw chicken into a wok. The steam engulfed his face.

"I've never seen anybody eat like these people. A bunch of spoiled hogs. Remember when we used to dig through the dumpsters together?" Juan would never forget it. Him and his cousin, too young to work, hungry. And as hungry as Juan was now, the thought of eating that Chinese slop that the Americans were gorging themselves with made his stomach churn. With his first check, he'd cook enchiladas. Chicken and sour cream. Black beans and rice. His mouth watered and he nearly drooled on himself.

"I told you, man. It didn't used to be like this. It was just me and Consuelo," Manuel said, pointing to an even fatter Mexican across the room. "Now, we can barely keep up with these fucking pigs. Whatever Mr. Chan changed in his recipe, it's like magic, man."

Just then, Mr. Chan stormed into the kitchen, his face stretched tight across his skull. His mouth was a straight line, razor thin, and his eyes pierced Juan. "Get outside. More tables need cleaning." He turned on Manuel. "You say your cousin good worker. He lazy Mexican, just like the rest. I fire you both!"

Juan couldn't make himself look at the little Asian man. His eyes found a stain on the floor and they stayed there. He saw Manuel's feet shuffling nervously.

The fading Chinese gibberish and the quick retreating footsteps let Juan know it was safe. He looked at Manuel with an open mouth. His mustache twitched.

Manuel shrugged. "He's a mother fucker, but he pays. I think you should get out there, cousin."

Juan dumped the dishes in the sink to the displeasure of the squat, elderly man standing there, whose hands looked like that of a body found floating in the river. Juan tried to smile, but the man's stare melted it.

Juan grabbed his cart and pushed it toward the door. He looked over at Manuel who was stuffing an eggroll into his mouth while he cooked. Bits of fried flakes drifted into his wok along with drips of his sweat.

"Come get one of these while the chink isn't looking."

Juan's stomach did a back flip at the thought of sustenance, but he wouldn't dare eat that food. He shook his head. "Let's stop by the store tonight after work. I'll cook us some food, just like I did back home, yes?"

Manuel furrowed his brow as if Juan's statement hurt his feelings. He shoved the rest of the eggroll into his mouth and looked like he swallowed it without chewing. "Whatever you say, cousin."

Shouting erupted from the dining room. Every worker in the kitchen stopped what they were doing and craned their necks to see through the cloudy plastic windows in the swinging doors. Chinese shouting and arguing exploded, and what sounded to Juan like grunting.

Juan turned to share questionable looks with Manuel, but his cousin was too busy stuffing as much food into his mouth as he could while the others were diverted.

When the scream rang out, it got Manuel's attention too.

30

KEEPING IT TOGETHER

As they cruised their assigned blocks, Jennings's gaze kept creeping toward Lola's thighs. She could feel the irises peeling back the fabric and taking in her flesh. It felt like maggots writhing and roiling over her, and she shifted uncomfortably so Jennings would hopefully get the idea and stop…but he didn't.

His eyes, set deep in his fat covered face, rolled up her stomach and landed on her breasts, stayed there for a vacation. He did nothing to hide it, even smiled and ran his tongue over his teeth.

Will this fucking light ever turn?

It clicked to green and the cruiser shot forward, Jennings's eyes finding the road again. Lola could have pulled her gun from her holster right then, cradled it between two of his chins, and emptied the whole fucking magazine. She stared out the passenger window and took deep, calming breaths.

"You hungry?" Jennings said.

"We just had lunch an hour ago." Lola kept her eyes on the world outside of the vehicle. A man walking his dog waved, but she only glared back.

"I'm still hungry. Whattya say we make a quick stop, huh?"

Lola massaged her temples and ground her teeth. "Why don't we do our jobs instead?"

Jennings snorted, pulled the car to the curb. He tried to turn to face her, but couldn't get his body to turn that way, so he tilted his head and grinned, showing his crooked yellow teeth. "Our jobs? And who the fuck're you to tell me what my job is, hm? Some fuckin' spick broad gets in my cruiser and tells me what to do?"

"Excuse me?" The headache that she'd been concentrating

on keeping at bay burst free and rammed against the inside of her skull.

"You heard me, bitch. What, did I hurt your feelings?"

As Lola glared at him, Jennings's face swam in her vision and began contorting into her father's. The bulges and rolls of unshaved fat melted into the sore-covered, glazed flesh of Daddy.

"Reach over here and rub Daddy's tummy, baby. Daddy don't feel good."

Lola clenched her teeth and turned her gaze to the floorboard. She breathed in through her nose, catching the spoiled scent of her father's bed sores, then out through her mouth. She grabbed her knees and squeezed, tried to force them to stop shaking.

"Lookey what we got here. Want me to do my job, honey?" The car bounced as Jennings wrestled with his seatbelt, then swung his door out and stood.

Lola didn't know what he was doing at first, but then she saw the girl, standing with her back against the brick building, chewing gum with an open mouth. The girl rolled her eyes and stood with arms akimbo as Jennings approached her: light-skinned and Hispanic, couldn't have been older than nineteen. Her skirt was just about crotch length and there was no question what she was doing on that corner.

Lola went to open her door, but Jennings put his fat ass in the way. His body eclipsed the girl and the building behind her, so Lola could only listen.

"What'd I tell you about this, Star? Thought I taught you a lesson last time."

"I ain't botherin' nobody, man. Just mindin' my own business." Though the girl had attitude, her voice could have been that of a cartoon mouse.

"Is that right?"

Jennings lifted his posterior off the car and Lola saw the girl, Star, back away. Her eyes searched around as if looking for an escape route.

Then Jennings looked right at Lola...and winked. He grabbed Star's arm at the elbow and swung her body around the front of him. He slammed her against the hood of the cruiser, the girl's ass sticking straight up and at him.

"What the fuck, man?" Every time Star tried to turn, Jennings forced her back down. Then his other hand found her ass.

Lola had enough. She wouldn't stand by while a young girl was molested by this fat son of a bitch—just to prove a point to her. She got out of the car, one hand on her gun. "Jennings, what the hell are you doing?"

"This little spick bitch has given me a lot of trouble. I've given her enough chances." His hand probed around under the girl's skirt, cupping in places, rubbing others.

Lola saw herself bent over the police cruiser, her father running his sticky, filth-covered hands over her body. Star clicked her tongue and widened her nostrils, didn't seem quite as appalled as Lola felt watching it. And the look on Jennings's face as he felt around, his heavy breathing, a slight phlegm-rattle in his throat, made Lola grip her pistol harder. Sweat beads rolled down his reddening face.

"That's enough, goddamnit." Lola made a move to stop him, to snap his wrist, pull his arm back behind him so far, he could tickle the fat folds on the back of his neck. But she stopped in her tracks.

"That shit ain't mine, man." Star struggled beneath Jennings's thick arm.

Jennings smiled as he showed Lola the crack pipe and bag of rocks. "And the little fucker is out here sellin' pussy. Can't have that, can we?"

"Look, take it easy," Lola said. "We'll take her in. I'll finish searching her, okay?" Lola couldn't stand to watch this obese prick lay his hog hands on this girl for another second, regardless of what she was doing. Nobody deserved that.

The girl turned her head and made a face like a little girl begging her parents for a toy. "Come on, man. Can't we work something out?"

"Watch your mouth, girl. You're in enough trouble as it is," Lola said. She nudged Jennings aside with her hip and took hold of the girl's wrists. Lola noted the satisfied grunt as her hip and leg brushed up against him, and a shudder ran up her body.

"Fuck you, bitch. I was talkin' to him." She nodded toward Jennings. "He loves getting his dick sucked, ain't that right?"

Lola raised an eyebrow and turned to face her superior officer. She expected him to laugh it off, tell the girl that telling lies would only get her in deeper trouble—something along those lines. But the fat fuck only smiled and seemed to be re-living some distant memory.

"Are you fucking kidding me, Jennings?"

"What, you believe her?" His words didn't match the smug look on his face. He bit his lip and locked eyes with Star.

"He knows it's true. Can hardly find his dick under all that fat. Just like lickin' a belly button." She laughed.

Under the circumstances, Lola almost laughed too.

"You little cunt. Let's see how funny you are after a few months behind bars, huh?" He moved forward like he was going to hit her and Lola shoved him back. Her open palm hit him square in the chest and she felt the air blow out of him.

He bared his teeth and his face glowed even redder. Sweat trickled down his head like grease on a roasting pig. "You'll be sorry for that. Just wait until we get back to the station, girl."

"Yeah, let's take this girl in, let her tell the Chief about your little extra-curricular activities. I think he might like to hear that." Lola let go of the girl's wrists, backed away.

Star turned around and glared at Jennings. "I got plenty of stories, man."

Jennings's confidence seemed to melt away. His eyes darted from Lola to Star to his feet, or his stomach, whichever he could see. "I don't need this shit." He stomped away, taking the drugs he'd confiscated, and slid back into the car.

"Thanks," Star said. "I wasn't lying, you know. But it got me outta trouble. More than once."

"I believe you," Lola said. "But we can't prove that. If I were you, I'd stay out of sight for a while. And next time I see you out here on this corner, I'll take you in myself. And there isn't anything to suck to get out of it either. Got it?" Star snorted, rubbed her wrists. "Yeah, whatever." She stalked down the street, swaying her hips and tossing her hair back and forth.

Lola knew she would catch hell as soon as she got back in the car, could feel Jennings's stare like laser beams melting the windows and hitting her in the chest. She peered into the passenger window but only saw his hands gripping the steering wheel, his hairy forearms twitching.

Come inside and sit with Daddy, honey.

Lola cringed, trying to force the thoughts out. Trying to keep herself from puking on the sidewalk as her mind played back the sight of jiggling fat, the smell of unwashed flesh, the sound of petroleum jelly squashing between hand and skin.

Give Daddy your hand, sweetheart.

Lola's hand could barely catch hold of the door handle. Her breaths came in ragged gasps, but she forced herself to get in the car, told herself that she would have her own squad car one day, that she wouldn't have to deal with this pudgy motherfucker for long, or any other pig-headed man. She just had to pay her dues first. *Take it easy. Be strong, you can take it.*

Jennings didn't mention a thing. He was too concentrated on the voice squawking from their radio.

"We've got an assault in progress at 5110 Humphrey Lane. The Paradise Buffet."

Jennings smiled as he struggled to face Lola. "There you go, darling. We get to eat *and* do our fucking jobs."

INSATIABLE

Juan moved past the other employees, who all seemed content with staying put in the kitchen, and out into the dining area. He looked over his shoulder, searching for Manuel, hoping his cousin would assist him. Still chewing, Manuel had moved his attention back to the food.

Mr. Chan shouted again, growled at someone.

"Manuel. Get the fuck over here," Juan said.

Manuel finally pried himself away from the food and trudged over.

Once Juan had taken in the scene, he needed the comfort of his cousin by his side before taking another step. He'd never seen anything like it.

A man, or what resembled a man, stood at the buffet line. His body was so wide, Juan couldn't see how he'd fit through the front door. What looked like blood covered his shirt, dark and dry, and was caked in the folds of his neck. His face was buried in a tray of food—what looked like beef covered in thick brown sauce—and his head jerked back and forth as he consumed it like a high-powered vacuum. He moaned as he ate, his hands in the neighboring trays, squashing noodles and pork into a pasty mush.

Mr. Chan held a bloodied hand to his chest, a cordless phone in the other. Blood dripped from a half-moon wound. He scowled at the beastly man gorging himself, then saw Juan and Manuel watching. "Do something! Do your job or you fired!" He winced and bared his teeth.

Juan looked around at the other customers and not one of them seemed interested in the chaos. They sat at their tables, the food on their plates the only concern, seeing or hearing nothing beyond their own little gluttonous worlds. Others walked around the man and scooped helpings of food onto their plates.

This has to be a joke. Manuel set this up to mess with me, some kind of initiation or something.

But Juan knew the little Chinaman was not acting. And Juan looked at his cousin beside him, who licked his lips and watched with earnestness.

"Police coming. *Get out of restaurant!*" Mr. Chan stomped his feet like a bratty child, blood pitter-pattering on the rug beneath him. He pocketed the phone, rushed forward, and grabbed the man's shoulder with his good hand. Juan could only imagine that was how his hand got bit in the first place. Mr. Chan bared his teeth as he tried tugging the man away from the buffet, looked like a flea trying to move a mountain.

Juan snapped out of his trance and jumped forward to help his boss. As he rounded on the fat man, Mr. Chan shot him a look of pure fire as if it were all Juan's fault. Juan grabbed the man's other shoulder and pulled. As his hands gripped, his fingers sunk into the soft, fatty flesh. The skin was slick with sweat and what appeared to be grease. Spots of dried blood speckled the skin and clothing here and there. The smell wafting from the bulbous body nearly induced a gag, but Juan held his breath and pulled, the cords in his neck ready to tear as he strained. He looked over at his cousin who hadn't moved an inch, still staring at the food in a dream-like wonder.

"Manuel, help me." Juan noticed that the other employees had disappeared back into the kitchen, not a single one of them in sight. "Manuel!"

His cousin blinked rapidly, glanced at Juan, and ran over. He took hold of the man's neck, his feet dangling off the ground for a second, then with all three of them pulling, they finally moved him. The fat man stumbled backward, pulled the metal dish—licked clean—from the buffet; it clanked to the floor. The trays where his hands were massaging the food fell and splattered the rug. Manuel barely avoided being crushed as the man slammed on his back.

The fat man grunted, his face a mess of color. He rolled back and forth like an overturned beetle. "More food...still hungry. It...it hurts." As he spoke, his tongue moved in and out, licking the sauce from his face. His breathing was wet and sloppy.

Sickness swelled in Juan's stomach and he backed away. The back of his thighs collided with a table, and he turned to find a couple, as fat as the fallen man, stuffing food into their mouths and staring up at Juan with blank, lost eyes. The woman rolled a fried chicken wing over her bottom teeth, stripping the meat and swallowing without chewing.

What is going on in here?

Juan shot a look at Mr. Chan, whose mouth was curved downward, eyes shifting all around at the diners in his restaurant. Juan could see panic in his eyes as they darted here and there. The little man held his hand to his chest and winced again. He looked at Juan, and for the first time, they shared a moment. It was the first time the Chinaman didn't look at him like a rat caught in a trap, but as an equal. Mr. Chan, out of all the people there, including Manuel, was the only other one that seemed perplexed by what was going on around him. Juan was glad to see that look because, for a moment, he thought maybe America was a giant pig trough. That maybe this is just how these people eat.

Manuel stood back and clutched his hands into fists at his sides. His stomach heaved as he watched the fat man on the floor, then his head turned in all directions to watch the other people eat their food. An animal savagery flooded his eyes. Juan wasn't looking at his cousin anymore, but some insatiable version of the man he once knew. Something had burrowed into his mind and was controlling him like a puppet—controlling everyone.

Mr. Chan edged toward Juan, then his softened features tightened back up into that sharp, angular sneer. "Do something."

Juan just looked at him and shrugged. As if there was a damn thing he could do. He felt like a worm in a tank full of starving fish. Sweat rolled from his armpits and tickled his sides.

The fat man on the ground finally rocked himself to his

hands and knees. He scuttled toward the spilled food, and with no hesitation, slammed his face into the thick pile and inhaled. The food disappeared and the man licked the greasy spot where it once was. His tongue, caked with partially chewed food, slid across the flat, blackened rug, the sound like sandpaper across wet concrete. Fat jiggled from side to side as he groaned and grunted. "Mmm…"

"Get up. Get out of restaurant," Mr. Chan said. "Where are fucking police?" The blood still gurgled and bubbled out of his hand, staining his shirt.

The fat man stopped, turned his head, his eyes landing on Mr. Chan. They locked there, the lids widening, nearly pushing the eyeballs out. His lips hung loose from his skull, dripped brown drool that puddled on the rug beneath him. He moved like a slug across the floor, rolls of fat cascading across his body in waves; he bared his teeth and wheezed, growled and snorted.

"Stay away," Mr. Chan said as he took blind steps backward. He glanced at Juan and pointed at the approaching man. "Stop him."

Juan looked all around and the diners still refused to acknowledge what was happening. The sounds of chewing and slurping filled the restaurant.

Juan ran forward and got between the shuffling pile of lard and his boss. The Chinaman sounded off behind him in rapid-fire Chinese.

"Food…more food…stomach hurts." With each word, he wiggled forward, snapping his teeth. His eyes were strained, the lids quivering. Veins bulged from his sweating forehead and around his eye-sockets.

"Stay back. Pinche cerdo," Juan said. With a moment of hesitation, Juan kicked the man square in the face. He felt the face squash against his shoe like he'd kicked a bag of marshmallows. Trickles of blood ran from the man's nostrils and faded in with the mess on his face. His tongue slithered out, sopped up the blood.

The man crawled under a table where a family of hogs shoved heaps of meat and saucy noodles into their maws.

The crawling fat man's face collided with the plump leg of the woman who sat there. Her chipped, red toenails sat atop toes that looked as spongy as Twinkies; the top of her foot bulged out of her sandal. She took no notice to the intruder-of-space under her table.

"H-hungry..." the man said, then bit into the woman's leg. He pulled away a chunk of stringy meat and chewed it with closed eyes. Blood pumped from the woman's leg... but she barely noticed. She winced when he bit her, looked toward the pain, then went right back to her plate. Blood rained on the man's head and he let his tongue hang out to catch as much as he could.

"Chingao..." Again, Juan looked for his cousin, but he was nowhere in sight. The double doors to the kitchen swung ever so gently, and Juan could just barely see violent movement back there.

Mr. Chan spat more Chinese gibberish at nobody in particular as he watched the bloody scene.

Red and blue lights flashed through the glass-front of the restaurant and illuminated the interior, turning the blood purple, then a brighter red.

The eaters didn't even flinch.

DADDIES EVERYWHERE

When they pulled up to the restaurant, Lola thought she'd sped into a nightmare. What she was seeing couldn't be real. As vivid as her dreams had been since the death of her father, it didn't seem too farfetched that she was really at home, passed out on the couch...or the floor.

A restaurant filled to bulging with...*Daddies.*

She saw her father's face on every fat body in the Paradise Buffet. And there were plenty of them. Sauce and grease glistened from their pudgy faces, dribbled down their layered chins. Shirts and pants stretched tight over blubbered bodies.

And they ate like they'd been starved for weeks. Lola could see the sloppy movement from her seat in the cruiser, the way their faces contorted and bloated as they chewed, some squeezing their eyes shut as if there wasn't enough room for eyes on their faces with all the food in their mouths. The hands worked fast though. Always moving, like lard-wrapped hummingbird wings.

I can't go in there.

"Let's get goin', girl. We got us a priority one here."

Jennings's voice was static in the distance as Lola shrunk into herself. Every one of the fat bastards in the restaurant, and the one right next to her, melted into a version of her father. She saw one Daddy in a flowery Mumu, plump feet stuffed into yellow flip-flops. Another Daddy tilted a bowl of soup and gulped it up, spilling it over his golf shirt, staining it brown. There were smaller versions of Daddy too, happily mashing food into their faces, using their chubby fingers as utensils.

She could hear them. *Come on inside, honey. We're waiting for you. Come give Daddy a kiss. Daddy's just so hungry.*

41

"No…no…no," she muttered as she brought her knees to her chest and wrapped her arms around them, rocked to and fro in her seat, her gun pressing into her hip. She thought she had herself under control, that she could keep the razor-sharp memories away for a while, but this was too much.

"What the fuck has gotten into you?"

Lola turned to face Jennings, but of course, Daddy stared back, dressed in a cop uniform. His tongue ran over his face, drinking in the sweat. His cheeks jiggled and glowed red.

What's the matter, baby? Aren't you glad to see me? I'm so hungry. I've been waiting for you to feed me!

Lola almost screamed, but caught herself just in time. She closed her eyes and breathed. I'm at work, she thought. On duty. *Get your fucking shit together!*

As much of a pig as Jennings was, he *was* her superior. If she showed any signs of weakness, showed that she couldn't handle the job, there was no question Jennings would report it to *his* superiors. And then she was screwed. Her job was all she had left.

"I'm…I'm fine. Let's move." And without turning her gaze back to Jennings, she popped her door open and jumped out. She jogged toward the front door of the restaurant, paused for another moment as she saw what was happening inside. She drew her gun and threw her shoulder into the glass, slamming it against the wall, then rushed inside, past the bubbling fish tank full of coy, and gasped when she faced the dining room.

A man lay on his stomach under a table just in front of her. It took every ounce of will she had to keep her mind from transforming him into her father. Blood coated his face and clothing. Some of it coagulated and dark, maybe a day old from the looks of it. The family above this man sat at the table and ate happily. As Lola took in the scene, the person who she assumed to be the man of the family stood up and headed toward the buffet which was bustling with other customers. The woman, a perfect ball with limbs, had a chunk of leg missing big enough to fit an apple into. Blood pumped from it rhythmically and washed over the fat man beneath her.

Then he opened his mouth as if to take a bite from the leg. Lola could only assume that he'd been the one to put that gaping hole in it, but she just couldn't imagine that was true. Why would this man bite into that woman's leg, and even more disturbing than that, why didn't she care?

"Don't move!" Lola pointed her gun, her finger shaking over the trigger.

The man didn't even know she was there, nor did anyone else in the restaurant. She had expected some kind of chaos when she arrived. Jennings had filled her in on the drive over, said a frantic "chink"—as he put it—had called complaining about a customer that refused to leave and how he'd bitten him on the hand.

She wondered where the chunk of leg was. If the man was emotionally disturbed, and bit this woman, surely he spit out the meat. But Lola didn't see it and the man, ignoring her orders, clamped his teeth over the woman's leg and bit down. He hit a different spot this time, tearing a fresh chunk away and...chewed on it. Before Lola could process what she was seeing, the man swallowed.

And the woman just ate and ate. She picked up her drink and let it run into her mouth and over her face and shirt, then went right back to eating. Her skin had already gone pale, and she lost more blood by the second, but she didn't seem to mind. The food was too important.

"Do something," came a high-pitched voice from her left.

Lola turned to see a Chinese man with a bloody hand pointing to the fat man and hopping up and down. A Mexican man stood beside him, his mustache twitching and his eyes darting from Lola to the Chinese man to the fat fuck on the floor.

Lola searched for her partner, but saw that he'd barely made it to the door. Sweat beads decorated his face.

She ran to the table, grabbed the woman by the arm. Just then, the chubby boy who sat at the table, oblivious to his mother being attacked and bleeding to death in front of him, got up and joined his father at the buffet line. Lola pulled the woman backward, who immediately thrashed and struggled to get back to her plate. Lola shoved her arms under the woman's armpits, and spun her away from the table.

"No...I'm not done. P-please...I need more."

"You're hurt, ma'am." Lola felt stupid for stating the obvious, but the woman truly didn't seem to know. Jennings was finally there and Lola passed the woman to him, told him to call an ambulance.

"And who the fuck're you to give orders?"

Lola noticed him smelling the air and she could have kicked him in the nuts right then. She didn't give him a response. As she turned toward the man on the floor, who licked up blood from the rug, she heard Jennings calling for EMS behind her.

Lola stepped toward the man, but not too close. If the son of a bitch laid a single finger on her, she didn't know if she could hold it together.

He looked up at her, his face knots and wrinkles of pain. His eyes bulged, his breaths whistled. "Please. Feed me."

"Put your hands behind your head." She said it because it came natural, but she knew he wouldn't listen. It didn't look like this guy could even reach the back of his head.

The customers should be rubber-necking now, she thought. Bystanders were usually incapable of ignoring the drama of an arrest. But no. Not even a wandering eye as far as she could tell. The air was alive with grotesque moaning, smacking, sucking, crunching. The chirps of utensils hitting ceramic were endless.

She knew she had to get out of there, knew a few more minutes meant the end of her very sanity. The contents of her stomach wanted badly to mingle with the woman's blood on the floor.

"Stay calm, ma'am. Help is on the way," Jennings said from behind, taking labored breaths as the words oozed from his lips.

"I'm...I'm not done. More food. More food!" The woman wrestled with Jennings, but his meaty arms kept her at bay.

All You Can Eat

Lola took a tentative step toward the pile of fat wriggling on the floor before her. His face pinched into a sneering grimace as she grew nearer. He reached for her, but his fingers wrapped around air.

"Sir, do not resist." She pulled out her mace, ready to burn the fucker's eyes right out of his skull if he took another swipe at her.

And he did. His teeth clicked like a bear trap.

Come down here and give your Daddy a little smoochy woochy.

She emptied the can dead center on his face. He made a sound like a pig drowning, but no sign of pain or even discomfort. His mouth opened and his tongue extended, and he drank the stream of liquid fire. Lola aimed for the eyes, hit them perfectly, yet he didn't flinch. He only strained harder to catch it.

"Arrest him. Get him out of restaurant." The Chinese man whined and tossed bits of his native language between orders. "Do something." He shoved the Mexican man in the back as if he wanted him to assist Lola in some way.

"No se," the bus boy said and side-stepped away from the frantic Asian. He locked eyes with Lola as if to ask if she wanted his assistance. His eyes kept darting around the room, hands wrestling with each other and feet shuffling.

Lola waved her hand, signaling for him to step back. The Asian man didn't agree and let loose with racial slurs and threats of termination. Even in the pandemonium, Lola felt sorry for the Hispanic bus boy. The sting of mace floated in the air, and Lola did her best to squint and hold her breath to lessen its assault on her senses. The two men became just as aware of it simultaneously and hid their faces behind the collars of their shirts. None of the others seemed to notice, which Lola didn't find surprising at that point.

She didn't see or hear the fat man climbing to his feet while she'd been momentarily distracted. Jennings didn't give any kind of warning, but he had his hands full with the woman as he continued to struggle with her. The woman growled and whimpered, her eyes on her unfinished plate of food. Her family had returned to the table with new plates, mountains of unrecognizable meat and fried things piled in front of them.

But Lola now had her full attention on the fat man covered in blood. He'd made it to his feet somehow, though it seemed impossible for him to have done so unassisted. He reached for her, mouth hanging open, rattling breaths dripping past dead-weight lips. The hair on his arms was matted down with blood and liquefied food.

"So...hungry."

"Don't do it. Stay back!"

"Hold still, lady. You're losing too much blood."

"I'm not done...not done."

"H-hungry..."

"Don't you take another fucking step."

"I fire you. Stupid wetback bus boy. Good for nothing."

"¿Que quieres que yo hago?"

Come to Daddy.

Lola went blind with rage. She'd been backing away, her gun back in her shaking hands, held out in front of her with unsteady arms. The man took thundering steps, each one sending tsunamis of fat rippling over his tremendous gut.

She holstered her gun and went for him. An open-palm was thrust into his sternum, but it felt like slapping a water balloon filled with pudding.

And he reacted with clicking teeth, missed her hand by a few inches.

She spun, cracking an elbow to the back of his head.

He stumbled forward just a bit—groaned wetly.

The heel of her shoe cracked the back of one knee, then the other.

He fell, sending a tremor through the floor that ran up Lola's legs and into her spine.

She jumped on him, pressed her knee to the pack of hotdogs that was the back of his neck, pushing with every ounce of strength she had to keep that mouth aimed at the floor. He tried to turn his head, but she kept him face-down, baring her teeth and grunting with exertion. She yanked the cuffs from her hip, snapped one end over his left wrist.

Getting his arm far enough behind his back to reach the other wrist proved to be a task for two.

"Jennings...help."

"Awe, fuck it." He released the woman who went right for her plate. Blood leaked from her wounds at just slightly a slower pace than before.

Jennings, slowly and clumsily, got down on one knee and wrenched the man's free arm behind his back toward the cuffs. With both Lola and Jennings pushing each arm toward the other, they just barely got them close enough to finish the cuff job.

Lola took lungfuls of air, soured by the scent of food and the sting of mace. Her chest heaved and she caught Jennings drinking in the up and down movement of her breasts. She was too exhausted to care.

"Not bad, kid. Now how do you suggest we get this fucker in the car, hmm?"

Lola had been thinking about just that at that moment. She couldn't lift the son of a bitch up, and she didn't want to risk getting bitten.

Then it hit her. She knew exactly what to do.

"Wait here."

She jumped up, ran to the closest table, grabbed a plate full of food to the displeasure of the elderly woman eating it. The wrinkled flesh of the woman's face jiggled as her gaze followed the plate in Lola's hand.

"Let him up," Lola said.

"You fuckin' crazy? We need back up." Jennings looked ready to pass out. His shirt was soaked in sweat, his hair pasted to his forehead.

"Just let him up."

Jennings didn't have a choice because the fat man caught a glimpse of what Lola carried just a few feet away from him and he tossed Jennings's fat ass away like a winter coat. He hobbled to his feet, with arms behind his back, and followed Lola as she crept backward.

"Come and get it, you fat fucking slob." She backed toward the door.

"Hey, what you doing?" The Chinese man shook his fist and peered at Lola with thin slits.

Once outside, Lola was thankful for the fresh air. The smell of that restaurant hit far too close to home for her. She backed toward the cruiser, taking quick glimpses over her shoulder to make sure she didn't step off a curb, twist her ankle, and become this lard ass's next meal.

"Give it...to me. I n-need it."

She threw the back door open and tossed the plate in, quickly stepped aside as the fat man crawled in after it, pushing himself forward with his knees. He slurped and moaned and Lola slammed the door. It hit something solid and came swinging back out, but Lola slammed it again, this time pressing her body against it until it clicked.

She collapsed to the pavement and watched the cruiser rock like it was filled with teenagers at a drive-in.

The ambulance zoomed into the parking lot and the EMTs ran by. One of them stopped. "You okay?"

"I'm fine. There's a woman inside with deep wounds on her leg. She's lost a considerable amount of blood. A man with a wounded hand too." The EMTs face swam in her vision and the parking lot behind him started spinning.

"You sure you're okay?"

"They really need you inside." She nearly told him about the others inside, the diners, stuffing themselves to the point of combustion.

The squeaking noise caught her attention and she looked back toward the car. The fat man had his face pressed against the other side of the window, running his tongue over the glass, smearing it with saliva and masticated meat bits.

Lola averted her gaze, took deep breaths, and fought off Daddy's voice as it crept back into her head.

AFTERMATH

As the paramedic wrapped Mr. Chan's hand, the Chinaman hollered and spat venomous words at the remaining customers. The kitchen had stopped producing food to fill the buffet with while the police were there.

Juan saw the Latina officer outside, leaning against the wall and talking to herself. The fat man had smeared blood on the inside of the car window as he stared out at her.

The portly officer with the hairy forearms questioned Juan and Mr. Chan. Juan knew the employees had disappeared because of the police presence. Hell, he wanted to hide too. The last thing he needed was to be deported back home before he had a chance to make any money. He could already hear his mother-in-law, screaming about how he was worthless, how her daughter deserved better. But the policeman seemed distant, scribbling mindlessly on his pad of paper as Mr. Chan babbled. The officer couldn't keep his eyes on the Chinaman or Juan; they kept peeling away to search the restaurant, his stomach grumbling, his mouth wet with saliva.

He had that look. The same look as the leg-biting fat man, the numbed-by-hunger woman…the rest of the people in the restaurant. The same look as Manuel.

Mr. Chan bounced and hollered for everyone to leave. Looking like Alzheimer's patients coming to consciousness while wandering the streets, the customers shuffled out. They'd eaten every bit of food that was on the buffet, every noodle, every loose pea. Licked up every drop of sauce. Some of them wandered from table to table, searching for any stray piece of food, but found nothing.

"Out. Get out. We closed," Mr. Chan said.

Bodies collided like bumper cars as they exited. Their eyes kept roaming to the empty tables and buffet behind

49

them, as if they were unable to accept that all the food was gone. They looked at each other, at Mr. Chan, at Juan with quivering eyes. Tongues slid over lips, hot burps exploded from throats, adding to the thick atmosphere of the restaurant.

When the last pig had left, and the EMTs gathered their equipment and exited, Mr. Chan locked the door, sat down and sighed. His hard demeanor faded and he seemed to lose himself in his thoughts.

Juan just stood there, unsure of what to do or say. He'd only known this man for a day, but he could tell that something heavy weighed him down. Mr. Chan looked up at Juan, and for a moment, looked ready to launch another verbal attack, but he just shook his head and buried his face in his shaking hands.

"It not supposed to be like this."

Juan wasn't sure if Mr. Chan said it to him or himself. He opened his mouth to speak, but didn't know how to say it in English, so he just clicked his tongue instead.

"I only want successful business. But not like this. It my fault...everything."

Juan shuffled his feet, shoved his hands in his pockets. The photo of his family wedged between his fingers and he pulled it out. He handed it to Mr. Chan. "I work for my family. They no here."

Mr. Chan's hand trembled as he held the photo, peered at it with those intense slits. His thumb bent the corner of the photo.

Juan took a step backward, not sure if he'd crossed the line. He clenched his teeth and braced himself.

But Mr. Chan wept. His sobbing sounded squeaky, like a dog toy with a hole in it. Pointy shoulders bounced and he gripped the photograph harder, creasing it. Juan could see him trying to collect himself, but the tears won the battle and refused to stop spilling. The way Mr. Chan was bent, leaned over with his elbows resting on his knees, the tears ran down his nose, met at the tip, swelled there before dropping and splashing on the rug, some of them dripping onto the photograph. Juan wanted nothing more than to snatch his

50

picture back.

"My wife…she leave me. For American," Mr. Chan said between sobs. He cleared his throat. "Restaurant doing bad. Food terrible. When no more money…she go. Leave me here." His face melted into a sharp frown. A tiny smile crept onto his mouth. "My grandfather, he live in China. So many successful restaurants. I ask him how. He give me…special recipe. Tell me people will love my food, but say be careful, say it very powerful."

Juan stood there, understanding just enough of Mr. Chan's words to get the gist of what he was saying. The little man no longer acknowledged Juan's presence, just speaking his thoughts out loud. He stared at the rug by his feet and giggled slightly.

"But I do it wrong. I use too much. It not supposed to be like this." Then just like that, he snapped out of it. He sat up straight, looked at Juan and furrowed his brow. He stared at the photo in his hand as if he'd just discovered it.

"Lo siento…sorry. You be okay." Juan smiled and tried to stop his mustache from twitching.

Mr. Chan snorted and tossed the photo away. It fluttered to the floor. "What? You clean now. Plates everywhere. Get to work." He stood, tossing the chair backward with the backs of his knees, and stomped toward his little office, spitting rapid Chinese phrases as he went.

Juan plucked the photo from the ground, smoothed out the bends and creases. He kissed his wife's face, then his daughter's. His lips came away damp from the tears that had coated the photo.

Peering toward the Chinaman's office, he curled one hand into a fist at his side, then took a deep breath and walked across the room to retrieve his bus cart. He piled plates, cups, and silverware into it, making sure not to let anything break. The last thing he needed was more shit from his boss, and he knew the little man wouldn't need much to set him off. So he did his job as quietly as he could. The plates had been licked clean, nearly to a sparkle, and he couldn't find a streak of sauce on any one of them.

Crashing and grunts from the kitchen caught his attention. With his cart filled, he wheeled it toward the double doors, but stopped short. He could hear it loud and clear now and his stomach dropped. Just like the customers, that unmistakable sound of gorging. The slurping and smacking and gulping and moaning. It pulsed from the kitchen and Juan hesitated before shoving the cart through the doors.

The staff, with Manuel in the lead, had piles of food laid out on the counter. They didn't say a word to each other as they stuffed the food into their mouths. Manuel dug into a silver bowl, pulling out handfuls of what looked like sesame chicken and mashing it into his mouth. Brown and orange sauce coated all their faces as they tore at the food like buzzards on a deer carcass.

The dishwasher—the squat, wrinkled man with a permanent-looking scowl—was on his hands and knees on the counter top, licking the chrome surface. He shuddered as if from orgasm as his tongue circled over the metal.

"Manuel…what are you doing, man?" Juan abandoned his cart and stalked toward his cousin. "What's gotten into you?"

Manuel's eyes landed on Juan, but there was no recognition there. He chewed like a grazing cow, his jaw moving rhythmically from left to right. His eyelids blinked slowly, then he lowered his head back to his food.

Juan grabbed Manuel by the shoulder, spun him around away from the counter. Manuel tried to turn back toward it, but Juan shoved him across the room, pinned him against the wall.

Manuel growled, snapped his teeth, nearly catching Juan's finger.

Juan slapped him, coating his palm in the sticky sauce that had covered his cousin's face. "Snap out of it, goddamnit. What's your fucking problem?"

Manuel continued to ignore him, stretched his neck to get another look at the food. The rest of the staff devoured what was left. Wet gasps filled the air.

"Manuel!"

Manuel blinked, looked into Juan's eyes. Something came back and Manuel crinkled his brow. He looked down at himself, then at his surroundings. "What's the matter?"

"What's the matter? Look at yourself."

Manuel held his hands in front of his face, gazed at them. He frowned at the mess that was there, then at the stains decorating his shirt. "What's going on?" A guttural rumble belched from his stomach, and Manuel nearly doubled over. "My *stomach*…"

The rest of the workers were oblivious to anything but the food, and some of them had wandered back into the cooler to get more. Juan concentrated on keeping his cousin grounded, tried to block the view of the others so he wouldn't snap back into whatever state of mind he was in. The state of mind that was common at the Paradise Buffet.

Manuel grimaced, leaned against the wall. "It hurts… ah, shit."

Juan patted him on the back, watched the others with a defensive eye. If any of those bastards started toward them, Juan would be running toward the knife block just to his right.

But the Mexicans didn't even know he was there.

The double doors swung in and slammed against the walls.

"What you doing? You steal from me!" Mr. Chan blew into the room like a hurricane. His feet collided with fallen silverware and metal bowls. He roared a stomach full of Chinese, then pounded his fists on the counter. "You fired! All of you fired."

Mr. Chan turned toward Juan and Manuel. He crossed his arms and stomped toward them. When he reached them, Juan side-stepped, leaving his cousin at the mercy of the Chinaman. Mr. Chan jabbed a finger in the middle of Manuel's chest, then wiped his finger on his pant leg. "You in charge back here. You…you fired too."

"Wait…Mr. Chan—" Manuel had wrapped his sticky fingers over Mr. Chan's arm, then winced and fell backward, clutching his mid-section.

Mr. Chan bent down, and for a moment, Juan thought he was showing concern for Manuel. But he unclipped a set of keys from Manuel's belt loop. "Steal from me? Get out! All of you!"

The rest of the staff still didn't comprehend what was going on, didn't have a clue their boss had just let them go. Mr. Chan picked up a mop that was propped against the wall and swung it like a bat toward the workers. The wooden handle whopped the dishwasher in the arm, then one of the former cooks in the chest. As he cracked the mop handle against each one of them, Juan saw their faces melt into confusion. They looked around the kitchen, at each other. Their eyes widened as Mr. Chan ushered them toward the back door, swinging his weapon.

"Fired. All of you. Get out!"

They began asking questions, pleading with their eyes, but Mr. Chan was deaf to their begging. Juan knew the job was the only thing keeping them afloat, or at least most of them. He understood. The job was the only thing he had, and he'd only had *that* for a day. If he was fired, he would be in worse shape than when he was in Mexico, broke with a void where his dignity had once been. But at least there, even with his mother-in-law barking insults into his ear, he had a family. In America, he had his cousin and a job. And his cousin was…changing.

Mr. Chan shooed them out the back, slammed the door, locked it. He tossed the mop away and sighed, then spun and faced Juan.

Here it comes. I'm next.

"You," Mr. Chan said. "Your cousin say you like to cook. You can cook?"

Juan glanced at Manuel who had worked his way back to his feet. His cousin clutched his stomach and leaned his posterior against the wall. "Uh…yes. I cook."

"Good." Mr. Chan tossed the keys to Juan. "You come early tomorrow. I find more workers. Mexicans all the same. You be here. Lots of work to do."

"What the fuck?" Manuel had his fists at his sides, the

54

veins in his arms bulging like wire under his skin. "I work hard for you. The food…something is wrong. You did this to me!"

Juan clutched the keys, felt them dig into his palm. Part of him wanted to rebel against this Chinese tyrant, to back up his cousin. But he pocketed the keys. His family was the most important thing, the only thing that truly mattered. Maybe he could help Manuel one day, but for now, he had to work.

"You get out of my restaurant."

"Fuck you. *Pinche chino*. You did it. You—" Manuel bared his teeth and whimpered. "The recipe. What did you do?"

Mr. Chan's eye twitched and he pursed his lips. He looked at Juan. "Get him out of kitchen. Be here in morning."

Juan stepped to his cousin's side, placed a gentle hand on his shoulder.

Manuel shrugged it off, spat on the floor, stormed out the back door.

Juan's mustache twitched and his eyes darted from the door to Mr. Chan. "What is in recipe?"

Mr. Chan frowned. Without answering, he headed toward the double doors back toward the dining area. Then he turned his head to face Juan. "Clean kitchen before you leave."

AMNESIA

It took every drop of Lola's will not to vomit inside of the patrol car as they drove the fat man back to the station. His smell alone turned the air hot and thick and made Lola want to ride on the hood: body odor and Chinese spice and old blood and the slight sting of mace. He pressed his chubby face against the cage between the front and rear seats and grunted, smacked his wet lips and ran his tongue over them.

"P-please...feed me. My stomach...it *hurts*." His breath was a fog of funk.

Jennings chewed happily in the driver's seat, steering with one knee as he double fisted fried chicken wings. Grease glazed his mouth and fingers. With every bite came a sickening crunch that sent quivers through Lola's body.

"Can't you wait til we get him booked?" Lola said. "Can't you see he's agitated?"

Jennings snorted and a tiny piece of meat stuck out from his nostril. He sucked it back in, chewed and swallowed. "I don't give a shit. If he's got him a little tummy ache, it's not my problem." He poured some sweet and sour sauce into his mouth, then stuffed a full strip of chicken in. "I'm hungry."

A dot of sauce catapulted from his mouth and landed on Lola's knee. She watched the fabric soak it up and she had to roll her window down before she blew stomach acid all over the console.

"You have to feed me. *I'm hungry!*" The man rubbed his face across the metal cage, grating his skin against it. Flakes of dried blood and sauce snowed down.

"Get your fat ass back," Jennings said, "before I pull over and whip your ass."

Lola couldn't look at either of them, had to roll her window down a few inches more, close her eyes, and take in

56

the fresh air. Her stomach rumbled and her mouth watered. She tried to escape in her mind, but Daddy was there waiting for her.

Daddy loves you, baby.

Her eyes burst open and she saw Jennings continue to eat through her peripheral. His hands worked fast to get the saucy meat into his maw and his jaw moved up and down in disgusting rhythm. The man slammed his body against the cage over and over, rocking the whole car as they sped down the road.

"Oh God...give me some food. Please. Just...just one bite."

Jennings laughed, his stomach bouncing in waves. He spat the mouthful of saliva-coated, mashed-up food into his hand, smashed it against the grating of the cage wall. "There you go, buddy. Knock yourself out."

The man didn't even hesitate. The brown glob plopped down onto the floorboard where it wiggled from the movement of tires over uneven pavement. The fat man tried to bend his body, like an obese contortionist, but couldn't even get close. His face glowed maroon, sweat oozed from pores, veins bulged to the point of bursting. Spittle rained from his purple lips as he growled and grunted.

"P-pull over." Lola had to concentrate to get the words out without spitting up.

Jennings watched through the rear view and chuckled. He crammed more food into his mouth.

The fat man, finally giving up on his struggle to slurp up the masticated meat, began licking the cage where the food had been pressed through. He snorted as his tongue slid roughly over the metal, moaning and whimpering.

"...Jennings...p-pull the fuck over." But it was too late. Her fat-fuck partner ignored her pleas and continued eating while he watched the man lick. Warm, frothy bile spewed past her teeth and lips, drenching her knees and the glove compartment.

"Jesus Christ, girl." Jennings's face pinched into a point surrounded by cheeks and chins. He picked up another chicken wing and bit into it.

Lola covered her mouth and breathed through her nose. She looked over at Jennings with watery eyes and her stomach gurgled as he chewed with an open mouth, strings of saliva connecting his top and bottom teeth, thick with mashed food bits.

Another stream of vomit burst from her mouth, spraying through her fingers and shooting off in all directions. Some of it hit her window and slid down in bubbly streams, some of it hit the ceiling, some of it hit Jennings on the chest and badge. One stream shot through the cage wall, splashing through the metal, and right into the waiting mouth of the fat man. He gulped it up and licked his chops.

"Goddamnit." Jennings hit the brakes and Lola nearly slammed face-first into the dash. While spitting strings of cuss words, Jennings swung his door open and stepped out of the car, still chewing. "Fucking spic bitch."

Lola heard the remark but was powerless to defend herself.

"*Mmmm.* I want more. Feed me...m-more..."

Lola fumbled with the door handle, slippery from her vomit, and finally got it open. She stumbled out and landed on the concrete with a thud. She scuttled away from the car as if the fat man would burst free from it and consume her. Broken glass bit into her palms, but the fear and disgust growing in her chest and stomach like spider webs of cancer took precedence.

"You'll be picking up the tab at the cleaners, you hear me?" Jennings stomped over, the Styrofoam box still in his hand. The son of a bitch was still eating.

It was then that Lola realized they were outside of the station. Her fellow officers walked by, smirking and elbowing each other. A couple of them made comments to Jennings and he laughed along with them—Lola the punchline.

She got to her feet, straightened her shirt and the front of her pants, and faced Jennings. "Sorry," she said. "Let's get this guy booked so I can get home." *I need a fucking cigarette.*

"I'll tell you what, lady. You get him inside and I'll finish my food." He placed his box on the hood of the car, plucked another wing and bit sloppily into it. "The little chink at the restaurant gave me a bag, and I'll be damned if it goes to waste."

Lola frowned, peered at the fat man through the car window. He sat still for the first time since they'd had him back there, his eyes darting all around, his head twisting from side to side.

"Please don't make me touch him…"

"It's the penalty for fucking blowing chunks all over me and my car," he said while chewing.

Lola wondered when the seemingly endless supply of chicken would run out. She hiccupped and winced at the sting in her throat. "How can you eat that shit?"

"What this?" he said and took another bite. "I'll tell you, that restaurant used to be shit. Little chink musta changed the recipe or something, cuz I can't stop eating it."

Lola stepped toward the vehicle, ignoring the wet, smacking ramblings of Jennings. The fat man saw her coming and glared at her as she approached.

Her hands wouldn't stay still, no matter how hard she squeezed them. The butterflies in her stomach had razor blades for wings.

Keep it together. Just do your job.

Come to Daddy, honey.

Lola wrapped her fingers around the door handle, popped it open, but not enough for the fat man to get out. "You're not gonna give me any trouble, right?"

His lip trembled and his eyes swam in tears. "W-what's going on?"

Lola's brow furrowed. "You're gonna play the amnesia card? Really?"

"I…I was hungry. M-my stomach…it… Why am I here?" The man looked around at his surroundings, taking deep, guttural breaths. He tried to look at himself, but could only see stomach. His eyes widened when they fell on the dried blood there.

"You really don't remember?"

"The buffet. I...I remember the food." Then his face contorted into a painful mess of skin and fat. "My wife... where is she? I remember...no. Oh God..."

Lola reached in, grabbed him by the crook of his elbow. He allowed her to pull him out without fussing. "We found you on the floor at the restaurant. You had bitten the owner on the hand and took a considerable chunk from a woman's leg. You were like...well, like an animal." Lola tried to stay professional, but doing so proved difficult. She walked him to the front of the station, ushered him inside.

The station buzzed with commotion. Conversations, shouting, shuffling papers, and the tapping of keyboards mixed together. The man's eyes darted in all directions, as sweat rolled down his messy face. He dragged his feet as Lola moved him along.

"The blood...my wife. You have to help my wife!" He spun on Lola and she almost went for her gun. *"Please..."*

"What about your wife?"

"At my house. She made me dinner. Oh God... My wife...I—" Tears streamed down his face, washing clean lines through the grime. The fat on his wrists bulged around the handcuffs like toothless mouths chewing on the metal. The skin was pink and torn in places.

"Let me get these for you." She knew it was probably against the rules, but she could tell this man was confused. He wasn't the monster she'd detained at the restaurant. Something was going on at the Paradise Buffet, something sinister. Lola imagined the little Chinese man cackling maniacally over a pot of bubbling concoction, sprinkling anciently evil ingredients into it to feed to the Americans.

Lola stood by the front desk, the clerk looking down at her and her hefty detainee with a smirk on his face. His cheeks bulged with food as he chewed. One hand scratched his chin, the other clutched a half-eaten burger.

Oh shit.

She felt the fat man tense up. One hand was already free from the cuffs, and she had a tight grip on it.

"*Hungry.*" The fat man reached for the burger, pulling Lola along with ease.

"What the hell are you doing?" the desk clerk said through a mouthful of food. He tried to scoot out of the way of the clutching hands, but he wasn't quick enough.

The fat man grabbed the officer by the collar and pulled him over the desk. The officer still clutched his sandwich, but it was quickly consumed by the obese attacker.

"Get off me!" The chewed up burger muffled his pleading.

"Let him go," Lola said, drawing her gun and aiming it at the jiggling mound of fat. Just as she expected, the fat man was oblivious to anything else but the food.

"Mmmm…"

The fat man swallowed and moaned. He had the officer pinned to the ground with the weight of his body and stretched his neck toward the man's face. The other officers in the station scrambled toward the ruckus, shouting orders and commands.

Lola knew she'd never hear the end of this. She wondered if she'd have a job after the events of the day. "Get off him, *now!*"

The fat man pressed his face against the officer's, and looked to be…kissing him. His moaning was louder than the officer's chokes and cries.

"Let him go, goddamnit." Lola's fingers ached from her hard grip on the gun.

The man looked up at her, chewing on the mushed-up burger that he'd extracted from the officer's mouth. Along with the man's raggedly torn lips. He got to his feet and swallowed the ball of meat, flesh, and bread, his tongue slithering and bathing in the food.

"*My face!*" the officer screamed from the floor, kicking his legs. He gurgled on his blood, choked on it.

The fat man licked his lips and his throat rattled. "*Mmmm.*"

He lunged.

Lola fired.

61

PAID

When Juan finished picking up and cleaning the kitchen, he headed out the double doors and into the dining area. Mr. Chan's voice exploded from the office by the entrance. Sharp, harsh Chinese sliced through the air. Juan wished he could just escape without saying another word to the little man, but he didn't want to risk pissing him off. He fired every employee there except Juan, so he knew the Chinaman had a hair-trigger temper.

As he approached the office, the words got louder, more violent. They tunneled into Juan's ears and cut at his brain. His mustache twitched as he poked his head into the office.

Mr. Chan had the phone pressed to the side of his face so hard, his cheek was pink and his knuckles were white. His eyes were perfect straight lines on his face, his eyebrows jumping and bending as he spoke. He paced the office, but when he saw Juan looking in, he sat down with his back to him and spoke softer, as if Juan had a clue of what he could be talking about.

He slammed the phone down, turned to face Juan. "You done?"

Juan nodded.

"I find more workers. That easy," Mr. Chan said. He stood up and grabbed Juan's arm. His fingers were like needles and cold to the touch. "You be here early in morning. Show me how good you cook."

After seeing the slop Mr. Chan had been serving the Americans, he had no worries that he could do the job. It was the one skill he was proud of. Sure, he'd never attempted anything even close to Chinese food, but he expected it would be no different than anything else, just different spices and sauces. He still felt pangs of guilt about Manuel losing his job. Then he remembered the look on Manuel's face as he gorged himself, and his guilt was replaced with fear.

Juan knew it wasn't Manuel's fault. There was something in the food that was changing people. Making them so hungry, they couldn't control themselves any more. It seemed a bit ridiculous to Juan that Mr. Chan would have some secret ingredient that was triggering the strange behavior, but he saw it with his own eyes: people turning cannibal, his own cousin—his best friend—hypnotized by hunger.

But Juan needed the job. Sure, the people were like zombies, but they loved the food so much, they couldn't stop themselves. And the man who bit Mr. Chan and the woman, he was just crazy. That's what Juan told himself over and over.

I need the money. My family needs me to work.

Juan shuffled his feet, found it hard to lift his eyes and direct them at his boss. "Mr. Chan? Can I have pay?"

When the Chinaman's eyes found Juan, they were like garbage disposals grinding up what little courage he had left. Then he smiled, though his eyes stayed hard as nails. He squatted to the metal safe by his desk, turned his body to block the view to the combination, then spun it to the left and right. He opened it, but just enough to get his hand in. Juan couldn't see what was in there. Mr. Chan closed it up, stood and faced Juan, a wad of folded money clutched in his bandaged hand.

"Here. You do good today. You be here early. Six o'clock." He handed the bills to Juan.

Juan hesitated as if the money were decorated with poisonous spines. His hand moved slowly through the air, then he snatched it out of Mr. Chan's hand like a toad's tongue catching a fly. "Thank you, sir."

"I see you in morning." Mr. Chan sat at his desk and ran his uninjured hand through is hair. He sighed and closed his eyes, remained so still, Juan thought he'd fallen asleep.

The photo of a woman in a chrome frame sat by the telephone. Pale skin, thin red lips bordering a mouthful of pearly teeth. She smiled sweetly from behind the glass.

"You still here?"

Without saying another word, Juan escaped the office and jogged toward the corner store. He bought a phone card and smiled as he imagined the soothing sound of his family's voice massaging his brain and melting the stress away. He'd decided he would also buy some fresh food and make him and Manuel the best goddamned enchilada dinner they'd ever had. His mouth watered in anticipation.

As he jogged across the parking lot, he noticed the fat bodies standing there like stone statues, the only movement the rising and falling of their chests as they panted. He recognized a few of the faces as customers he'd seen throughout the day. They just stared at the restaurant, taking no notice to anything going on around them. Some of them still had sauce coating their faces.

Pinche cerdos.

MONSTERS OF OBESITY

Lola inhaled deeply and fluttered her eyes as the smoke slid down her throat. The filter of the Marlboro was dented by her fore and middle fingers as she squeezed it to keep her hand from shaking. No matter how many times she spat or rinsed her mouth out, she couldn't get the sting of vomit out. It coated the interior like dead skin.

She still felt the violence of the gun in her hand, couldn't shake it off. The hand dangled limply at her side and she couldn't even look at it. It was the first time she'd ever fired her gun at anyone. A lot of officers go their whole careers without ever doing it, and here she was, a month in, already one kill notch on her belt.

The scene played itself over and over in her mind, and no matter what she did, she couldn't make it stop; even invited the memory of her father, but he didn't show. She saw the officer lying beneath the fat man, his mouth all gum and teeth, a bloody tongue swirling in the air like a tentacle. His limbs thrashed, the rubber of his shoes and his damp fingertips squeaking against the floor.

She saw the bullet enter the fat man's chest. Right between the tits. Ripples danced across the blubbery body. He still reached for Lola, the handcuffs dangling from his wrist. Just before he collapsed, just before his brain told the rest of him that he was dead, he gave Lola a look. A look that said, "How could you do this to me? You know this isn't my fault." And then he fell backward, smacked against the floor like a slab of beef. The lower half of his body landed on the officer's stomach and knocked the wind from him. The struggling officer's teeth clicked together as he gurgled and choked on his own blood.

Lola just stood there and stared. Her fellow officers

patted her on the back, congratulated her as if shooting the guy was some kind of rookie initiation.

But it's my fault. I shouldn't have taken the cuffs off.

As other officers struggled to move the now dead weight of the man off of the lipless officer, a deep rumbling made them retreat backward a step or two. The dead man's bowels, surely on the brink of exploding with all the food crammed into his stomach, let loose. The man's pants had fallen halfway down his ass, and thick, molten shit poured and sprayed past the beltline and onto the wriggling officer beneath. Brown liquid painted his exposed gums. It took nearly everybody in the station to roll that big son of a bitch off while their fellow officer hollered something awful. Lola could hear his screams even as the ambulance took him away.

Lola shook out the shiver in her spine and used the smoldering butt of her cigarette to light another. She'd been questioned, had to give a statement, but her supervisor told her to get home, that they would finish up tomorrow.

She wept through the whole ordeal, and only now, with the smooth smoke of the cigarette inflating her lungs, did she feel at ease. All she could think about was a hot shower, and she smiled and imagined the scalding water burning away the stink of the day.

But she couldn't make her legs work yet, just leaned against the brick wall of the station, taking in mouthful after mouthful of smoke. She still needed to punch out, but she was in no hurry to step foot back inside. The smell of shit hovered in there like dense fog.

The doors swung out and, even without turning to see who it was, she knew it was Jennings. His labored breathing and grunts of exertion as he walked his fat ass through the entrance announced his arrival. She could hear his tongue clicking as it stuck and unstuck to the roof of his mouth.

"Hey there, dead eye," he said, bumped her arm as he shuffled past to face her. "How bout we get a bite to eat, huh? On me."

"Are you fucking kidding me?" She almost jammed her cigarette into his sunken eye.

"I'm starved. Thought I'd be nice, extend an invitation."
He massaged his stomach and swallowed a mouthful of spit.

"Is that all you ever do is eat? Makes me fucking sick,"
Lola said as she stomped her cigarette out. "And I could've
used some help. Too busy stuffing Chinese food into that
hole on your fat head." Even though her face burned with
embarrassment from her harsh words, it felt damn good to
feel them catapult from her lips. She kept her eyes hard as
she looked up from her crushed cigarette to Jennings's face.

But her superior officer didn't even acknowledge the
insult. His eyes had gone blank, lips hanging from his face
and glistening with saliva. The rumbling of his stomach
sounded like a passing semi.

"Jennings?"

"I'm...hungry."

Lola turned when she heard the scraping of shoes against
the sidewalk. A man walked by, thumbing the screen of his
cell phone, a sandwich in his other hand. Meat flapped from
between the bread as he walked, and without looking away
from his phone, he took a bite.

Jennings grunted and ran his tongue over his plump,
pink lips. His head swiveled and his eyes stayed pinned on
the man as he went by. Without another word to Lola, he
followed the man down the sidewalk. The sandwich man
had no idea he was being pursued, and Lola had flashes of
the fat man in the restaurant, flaying the meat away from the
woman's leg with his teeth.

She tried not to let her imagination wander and ran her
fingers through her hair. The nails scraping against her scalp
felt good. Her eyelids slid shut and she let her weight sag
against the brick wall behind her.

What the hell is going on around here?

One crazy, fat bastard running amok in an all you can
eat buffet—she could wrap her mind around that. But a
restaurant stacked with monsters of obesity, too entranced
by the food on their plates to even recognize an act of
cannibalism happening right beside them—every one of
them with that nothing-going-on-upstairs look—was too

weird to be a coincidence. And the woman, oblivious to the pain in her leg, the pints of blood she was losing, more concerned with shoving more food down her gullet.

And now her own partner. As long as she'd known him, he'd always been a fat ass, but he had that *look* now. She genuinely worried for the sandwich man.

"Got any money? We're starving, officer."

Lola rolled her eyes open, expecting an emaciated transient with tattered clothing, matted facial hair, maybe a rotten odor. But when she saw what stood before her, she crinkled her brow and stood up straighter. She felt like she was trapped in a Stephen King novel or something.

A family of four. Dressed well enough, like any middle class family she supposed. But fat. Every one of them. Besides what looked like sauce stains of some kind, their clothes looked clean. They hadn't been living in the street, she could tell that right away. But the longing in their eyes, the hopelessness in their faces—they were like the others.

Her hand, the murderous one, went toward her holster instinctively, but found nothing. The weapon was now evidence and she was left defenseless if this family decided she looked like a chicken dinner. Then, as her brain slowed down and her adrenal gland settled, she felt silly. A portly man and woman with their two kids.

Motherfucker, will this day ever end?

"Sir, do you guys need some help?"

The woman stepped forward. "Please, we need money. We have to eat."

The rest of the family nodded. The kids' eyes scanned the ground, Lola assumed for fallen change, but they licked their lips. She could hear their stomachs like distant thunderstorms. The boy bent down, plucked a black leather wallet from the street. The family's eyes widened and they surrounded the boy as he searched it, but found nothing worthwhile and tossed it away. They sighed together.

"Why don't I give you folks a ride home, hm?" She stepped forward and placed a gentle hand on the little girl's back. The girl spun, her mouth open, teeth bared. Lola snapped her hand back and stared at the girl, awestruck, and then the girl went back to searching the street.

"We don't need to go home. It's the buffet we want. We need it," the man said.

The family nodded.

"What did you say?"

"The buffet. We ran out of time...ran out of money. We're in *pain.*"

"Can you help us?" the boy said.

"I...I don't have any money. You folks should get on home." Her eyes darted from person to person and the knot in her chest tightened. She held her breath as she watched the family sink in disappointment.

They moved along, bouncing their bulbous bodies down the street, searching the ground together. Nobody spoke to one another. They stopped just a block away, faced a couple that were walking down the sidewalk, pleaded with them for money.

Jesus Christ.

Lola walked into the street and grabbed the wallet. She flipped it open, didn't recognize the handsome face on the driver's license at first, the type of face to make any woman blush and check her breath. It was the eyes that gave him away. The wallet must have fallen from his pants as she pulled him out of the car.

The man had said something about his wife, she remembered that now. When the animalistic fury had faded from his eyes and he was human for just those few minutes, he seemed to remember something that chilled him to the marrow. He'd wanted Lola to help her.

What if she's hurt? What if she's dead?

Lola didn't know which she preferred. If she was alive, Lola would have to explain to the woman that her husband was killed, that he'd been chewing on people and that Lola had to put a bullet in him. But Lola knew the woman would be nothing more than stripped bones and bloody clothing. The congealed blood coating the man's face and clothes made sense now.

She pulled the license out, pocketed it, tossed the wallet into the wastebasket beside her.

She felt she owed it to the man whose body lay cold and lifeless in the morgue. As bad as she felt she needed it, that shower was going to have to wait.

TASTE JUST LIKE STRAWBERRIES

Juan trudged down the sidewalk, the bags of groceries swinging by his sides. It was a good thing Manuel's apartment was only a few blocks away from the restaurant, otherwise Juan would have been lost.

The phone card was burning a hole in his pocket, and he couldn't wait to hear his family's voices, even though he knew he'd have to get through his mother-in-law to get to them. He didn't care. She could call him every name in the book, could insult him until his ear bled. As long as he heard the sweetness of his wife's voice and the squeaky, innocent voice of his daughter, all would be well.

He'd bought plenty of food for him and Manuel; decided to make Enchiladas Verdes, his personal favorite. The grocery list consisted of four chicken breasts, a pound of tomatillos, two white onions, five Serrano peppers, two cloves of garlic, a bunch of cilantro, and a dozen corn tortillas. He also bought a case of Pacifico to show Manuel he was sorry for what had happened. Juan hoped his cousin understood that he needed the job and that the situation was out of his hands, and he'd already decided that he would give Manuel a bit of money here and there—he owed him anyway.

Juan was excited to show Manuel what he'd brought for dinner. He'd hoped they could feast on some real food, not that pig slop Manuel had been eating, and knock a few back while they reminisced about their childhood together. Always the best of friends, always watching out for each other. Juan needed Manuel to understand that nothing that happened today was anything personal. That if he had a choice, Juan would have spit in Mr. Chan's eye.

As he walked through the parking lot, a Mexican girl that looked skinny enough to pick his teeth with approached him.

Hard nipples poked against her tattered t-shirt. She smiled and revealed a red streak of lipstick across her front teeth, which were the shape and color of raisins.

"Que paso, wey?" She bit her bottom lip, grabbed her crotch, and pressed her bony body against Juan. It was obvious she didn't actually speak fluent Spanish. "I'll suck your verga for twenty dollars."

Juan scrunched his brow and continued walking.

"Come on, man. Ten!"

He walked up to the apartment door, placed his groceries on the ground, but paused before wrapping his fingers around the doorknob. There were voices from inside. Grunting and moaning.

The scene from the buffet flickered in his mind. The fat man biting into the woman's leg like it was ham. The restaurant full of the people, eating mindlessly. Manuel and the rest of the staff as they stuffed themselves silly in the kitchen.

Hijo de puta.

Juan squeezed his eyes shut, said a quick, silent prayer, then swung the door inward.

A woman screamed.

Juan jumped and screamed too.

Manuel stood behind a scrawny white girl, ramming his brown cock into her with such violence, Juan was surprised the tip wasn't coming out of her mouth. Manuel looked over at Juan as he pumped and smiled slightly. He never slowed. The girl looked shocked, like she was momentarily embarrassed, but as Manuel rammed into her, she went back to her grunts and groans. Her ribs pressed against her wan skin and track marks ran across her arms like tattoos.

Juan stood there, frozen. He didn't know what he expected to find when he entered the apartment, and part of him was happy that Manuel was finding joy some way or another. Especially after losing his job. A job he'd held for over a year and lost on the very day Juan started.

But the look in Manuel's eye. That same animalistic look he had earlier. The smile split his face like a flesh wound.

Juan set down the groceries, closed the door. He wanted to get the food in the refrigerator so it wouldn't get ruined, but he couldn't get out of that apartment fast enough. Police sirens and distant arguments crashed through the air as Juan stared out into the parking lot.

I can't bring my family here, he thought. *They deserve better.* He would save enough money to get them a house, in a nice neighborhood somewhere. Where his daughter had a chance.

He walked across the parking lot again, passed the Mexican girl with the two ant bites for tits and the ten dollar boca. She squatted in front of a bush, a yellow stream trickling from between her frog-like legs. When she saw Juan, a smile stretched her face tight.

"Que paso, wey?"

Juan quickened his pace.

He went back toward the corner store where he'd picked up the groceries and phone card. A payphone erected from the concrete, inked with graffiti. An emaciated black man sat huddled behind the dumpster there, the whites of his eyes like neon lights. His body shook and he smiled as he placed the glass pipe to his lips.

Juan turned his back, leaned against the payphone, picked up the receiver. He typed in the phone number on the card, listened to the automated woman's voice until it asked for his pin, then pushed it in with an anxious finger. When prompted, he dialed his mother-in-law's number which he knew by heart. There was silence, and for a moment he nearly panicked. When it started ringing, his knees shook and his stomach roiled.

He shuffled from foot to foot as it continued to ring, and just as he was sure nobody was home, the gruff voice that he'd never been more happy to hear said, "Bueno."

"Hey, it's Juan. Is Claudia there?"

A long pause, then a rattling sigh. "You still remember her name, at least. How are the American whores treating you?"

Juan couldn't help but smile. "I've been doing nothing

but thinking about my family. I found a job and got a promotion on my first day. Already got my first pay."

Grunting, then a coughing fit. "Yeah, and I bet you hand that money right over to the first pussy you see. Or you'll drink it away. Or both. What do you want anyway?"

"Claudia. I want to speak to my wife." Juan's mustache twitched and he shoved his free hand into his pocket. "Please."

"Mama, who is it?" Juan heard the faint voice in the background. Then some shuffling and moving around. He could tell his mother-in-law was reluctant to hand over the phone. "Juan?"

"Hello, beautiful. How are you?"

"Oh, Juan. I, I miss you so bad. I was worried you'd been caught by border patrol or something."

"No, Manuel set me up pretty good. How's our baby girl?"

"A handful, of course. But Mama has been a huge help. I...I found a job."

Juan sighed. "I'll be sending you some money soon."

"I know. We just need a little extra to get by."

Juan's hand became sweaty and he had to grip the phone harder. "I love you. All I can think about is having you and our baby back in my arms. I...I miss you so goddamn much."

A sniffle. "Me too."

They went back and forth like that for a few minutes. Tears streamed down Juan's face and he felt more lost than he had before calling. He thought it would make him feel better, and to a degree, it did. But hearing Claudia, and sensing the sadness in her, Juan never felt more far away.

"Would you like to speak to your daughter?"

"More than anything."

A short pause that felt like a lifetime. "Daddy?"

"Hi, baby. What are you doing?"

"I brush my teeth. Grandma said you're not coming back."

Juan wanted to bash the receiver into the middle of the hag's face. He wondered what other poison she'd been dripping into his daughter's ear.

"It's not true, baby. Daddy will be bringing you to a new home. Soon, okay?"

"Okay. I don't like it here. Grandma smells and she farts when she sleeps."

Juan laughed and cried at the same time. "You be good. I love you and miss you, baby."

"Love you too, Daddy."

"Juan?" Claudia again. Juan could tell she had wept while he spoke to their daughter.

"Yes."

"I have to go. I need to wash her and get her to bed. And I have work in the morning."

"Okay." He wanted to say more but couldn't.

"I love you. We'll be thinking about you."

"I...I love you too." Before he could say anything else, she was gone. He kept the phone to his ear as the dial tone came on. Wet tear stains polka-dotted the concrete between his shoes, and he watched as more pitter pattered there.

A tap on the shoulder.

Juan ignored it and ran his forearm over his eyes. His mustache was slick with snot. A weak hand hung the phone back on the cradle, and he took a long, deep breath.

Another tap. "Say, ese. You got some change?"

Juan turned to find the skinny, pipe-sucking black man there. His eyes had cataracts and his front teeth were missing. Two yellow teeth hung past his top lip and made him look like a vampire.

Juan just shook his head. He started to walk away.

"Come on, holmes. Anything. I'll suck your dick."

Juan saw red. He stepped up to the man and shoved him dead in the chest. The man stumbled on his twig legs, crashed into the stone wall of the store, cracking his head against it. The man crumbled into a heap and covered himself.

"Motherfucker." Juan stomped and kicked. The man turned into his mother-in-law, then Mr. Chan, then Manuel, then the coyote. He became the fat fucks from the restaurant.

"Stop. Please...leave me alone." The man pissed on himself and sat in a spreading pool. A lamp shone sickly,

75

jaundiced light down on him, junebugs and moths swirling around him and clicking when they hit the wall. His body shook and he gasped, his hands held out in surrender. "I'm sorry...I'm sorry."

Juan backed away. He blinked rapidly, his mustache twitching out of control.

What the fuck is wrong with me?

He jogged away, back toward the apartment, and hoped Manuel was finished. Whether his cousin was done or not, Juan decided he needed to start cooking their dinner. Preparing the food would get his mind off things, would calm him down. His stomach begged him for sustenance.

The Mexican girl was there, waiting for him. He shook his head frantically as he passed her, didn't want to hear another word ooze from her disease-ridden mouth.

"Well fuck you then!" she shouted.

Juan went straight for the apartment door. More moaning from inside, a wet sound squishing in the air.

I don't care. I'll just turn my back to them.

He threw the door open. His jaw felt like it weighed a hundred pounds as he stared into the efficiency.

"...Manuel...w-what..."

Manuel ignored him as he bit into the woman's body again. Her stomach was torn to shreds, purple and pink hanging out like party favors. White ribs shone from the mess of red. Manuel tore a hunk of flesh away from her chest and swallowed it whole.

Juan covered his mouth with his hand, and couldn't stop his entire body from shaking.

FAMILY DINNER

Butter fell off in clumps as Timothy stuffed handfuls of it into his pink mouth. The tub sat between his legs on the kitchen floor. Gwen slurped up raw slices of bacon, barely chewing before swallowing. The kids took no notice of each other. The refrigerator and freezer doors hung open. Chubby fingers reached for food—any food—and brought it crashing to the tile beneath before being devoured.

Dad sat at the kitchen table with a frozen whole chicken, clawed at the icy flesh, licked the beady skin. He bit into the breast and tore away a chunk of meat, chewed on it with difficulty.

Mom chased the cat around the living room, her torso bouncing up and down and to the side, her breasts battling each other under her stained blouse.

The kids grunted and breathed heavily as they emptied the contents of the refrigerator down their gullets. They made quick work of it, hardly chewing anything, letting it sit on their tongue long enough to get a quick taste, just a smidgeon, then down it went. Timothy stuffed raw egg after raw egg into his mouth, the shells crunching between his teeth like sand.

He couldn't remember how things got the way they were. It seemed just weeks ago, they were a happy, normal family. Him and Gwen battled for the "best report card" spot on the fridge door, held there by the magnet shaped like a graduation cap. Mom and Dad loved them, supported them, provided for them. Times were rough, Timothy knew that. Money wasn't easy to come by he had heard Dad say a few times.

But Timothy's birthday came up. They always go out on birthdays—a family tradition. That year, Timothy had discovered his love for Chinese, sesame chicken in particular.

"How bout the Paradise Buffet?"

And they went, the whole family. And they ate. Then ate some more. And more. The food was amazing. Timothy couldn't stop. But after an hour, they were forced out. The next day, Dad piled everyone into the van and they went back. Then the day after that. It started to haunt Timothy's dreams, his every waking moment. He wasn't thinking about the food...his thoughts *became* the food. Like his brain was deep fried and floating in sauce. It got to the point that nothing would satisfy him, and from the looks of it, the rest of his family felt the same way.

Nobody cared about grades any more. Nobody cared about anything except the Paradise Buffet. Their stomachs churned uncontrollably. No matter how much they ate, it wouldn't fix the hunger. And they grew, every one of them. Bulged and widened. But they only craved the Paradise Buffet. The other food was to calm the guttural growls in their bellies, just to hold them over until they could get back to the buffet. But they had no money. It was gone. The Chinese man wouldn't let them inside without money. No matter how much Dad and Mom begged.

There were others too—like them. Fat. Begging.

So the scavenging of the house began. Anything to make the pain go away.

Timothy looked at his sister, who bit into a block of Velveeta, chunks of meat and condiment splashed over her face. He reached for the cheese, kicking the empty butter tub away.

"No," she said, turned her shoulder, bit into the cheese again.

Timothy looked into the refrigerator, frowned at its empty shelves. He pulled down the milk jug and upended it down his throat. The cold liquid splashed over his face, poured into his nostrils, nearly choking him, but he gulped it down. He looked at Gwen who deep-throated the last of the cheese.

Together, they ruffled through the freezer, finding only

chips of ice and empty packages.

"*Still hungry...*" Dad stood up from the table, picking at the chicken bones with his finger. He looked toward the kids and growled.

Mom couldn't move fast enough to catch the cat and she entered the kitchen with clenched teeth and curled fists. Mascara ran down her face in black crooked lines.

Timothy reached toward his sister, plucked a piece of meat from her chin, sucked it from his finger.

Dad rampaged toward the shelves, found them empty, roared and slammed his fists on the counter.

Mom fell to her knees, weeping. She lay on her stomach, slamming her face into the floor over and over, kicking and slapping the tile. A small pool of blood formed, leaking from the crack on her forehead. She licked it—moaned. The cat prodded toward her, sniffed at her ankle. Mom shot a bloated hand out, grabbed hold of the tail. The cat yowled, screeched, turned and latched its claws deep in skin and fat. But Mom didn't react. She had one hand wrapped around the tail, the other on the throat. Talons scraped and gouged her face, yet she pushed her mouth closer, clamped teeth over fur. The yowls turned to screams. Dad thundered toward Mom, slid on his knees to join her. The cat didn't make any more sounds, but Timothy heard Mom and Dad crunching and sucking. And he was jealous.

He looked at Gwen again.

She looked at him.

It was a head on collision, both grabbing whatever they could on the other. Timothy felt a sting on his arm, the bendy part opposite his elbow, as Gwen chewed into it. He sunk his teeth into the back of her neck, yanking and pulling meat and hair away from the rest of her. The succulence in his mouth outweighed the hot pain in his arm.

They both chewed—swallowed. And were back at each other.

Gwen bit the side of Timothy's head, ripped his right ear away like a strip of jerky. She tried to scoot back to eat in peace, but Timothy got hold of her ankle, yanked her back toward him. He bit into the bottom of her foot, feeling the satisfying plunge of his teeth into the warm meat—pulled his incisors down and flayed the flesh away in a thick strip.

His sister wailed while her foot slapped against the tile, wet like a seal's flipper, splashing blood. Gwen reached for Timothy, trying to get to the fleshy treat hanging from his teeth. She bit down on the other end of it, and they tugged in opposite directions until the meat ripped in half.

And Timothy went for more. Gwen was busy chewing. He bit into her calf. She grunted but still chewed.

"*It's mine...*" Dad stomped across the kitchen to join in on the feast. Black and white bits of fur were pasted to his lips and chin with blood.

Timothy took another mouthful of leg, tore it away with a swinging of his neck. Gwen tried to sit up, either to stop him from hurting her further or to try and take the meat from his mouth. But Dad caught her by the hair, swung her head back to the floor with a crack.

He chewed on her face like a man in a pie eating contest, swinging his head back and forth as he gorged. When he pulled away, Timothy saw that Dad's nose was gone, now a hole pouring blood onto Gwen's face and chest. She chewed on it, crushing the cartilage and skin, wincing as Timothy took another bite from her leg.

With an *umph* and a clicking of the teeth, Mom dove across the floor and went for Gwen's other thigh.

Gwen gurgled and tried to thrash, but the weight of the family was too great. Her head rolled in place.

Then Dad went for the stomach, the rolls and rolls of glorious fat inviting him. He shoved his head into it and frenzied. Blood and fat poured forth, red and yellow. The yellow was sticky, gave off a scent that made Timothy's mouth water even more. He joined Dad, then Mom did too. Even Gwen reached down, grabbing handfuls, stuffing it into her mouth and groaning with a mixture of pleasure and pain.

The growling of stomachs mixed with the wet sloppy sounds of eating.

They all paused, just for a moment. Timothy and Gwen

glared at each other. Dad and Mom looked at themselves, frowned, then at each other, mouths agape, dripping with gore. It was as if they all realized, just for a fraction of a millisecond, that something was wrong.

Gwen whimpered, her lips quivering between gasps.

It was like a dinner bell.

In unison, as a family, they continued their meal.

I NEED IT

Juan slammed the door, pressed his back against it. Manuel shuddered as he stuffed bloody meat and sloppy viscera into his mouth. The woman's face was petrified into a mask of torment and sadness. Her tongue hung over the corner of her mouth like rotted fruit. One of her small breasts had been torn away, replaced by a ragged, yellow patch. She'd been devoured from the bottom of the ribs down to her sex, which was no longer recognizable as a human part. Looked more like chili meat. Manuel sat Indian style in a pool of blood and gore, naked, his manhood painted red, smacking as he chewed.

"M-manuel. Stop." Juan heard his own voice, but couldn't remember speaking. He felt a trickle of warmth run down his leg.

Manuel's head snapped toward Juan, flinging blood from his mouth.

Juan tensed. He pictured Manuel snarling like a rabid dog and lunging for him. But his cousin's eyes drooped and his lips trembled.

"My stomach…it hurts so bad. The *pain*. I don't have a ch-choice…I have to eat." He turned back to the hooker's body and jammed his face into her stomach cavity, rolled his head and slurped up the soupy mess.

Juan gagged, burped, held his quivering hand over his mouth. "Manuel…cousin. You have to stop."

"The buffet. M-Mr. Chan's food. I, I need it. *I fucking need it!*" He reached up, grabbed the girl's head by the hair, pulled it toward him. His bloody jaws bit into her cheek right below the eye, peeled off a piece the size of a pancake. It wiggled from his mouth as he chewed. His cheeks bulged with meat.

Juan took a step forward. The floor was slippery with gory chunks. He placed a hand on Manuel's shoulder. "I...I'll take you. To the restaurant. Just fucking stop."

"Yes. Yes, the restaurant. The buffet." Chewed meat spilled from his mouth as he spoke. "You'll take me there, right, cousin? Y-you take me."

Warm tears crept from Juan's lids and the sting of bile assaulted his throat and nostrils. He glimpsed at the corpse without meaning to. So much of her eaten already. Manuel's stomach bulged and looked hard.

"Yeah, I'll take you." Juan felt the keys poke his thigh from inside of his pocket. He wondered if Mr. Chan was still there. If he was, Juan was ready to kill him. People don't act this way. His cousin was not this cannibalistic monster before him. Manuel was a good man, a loyal friend. Had the guts to leave his home and travel into an unknown world where his kind was treated like rats, where they spoke a different language, where they give you the hardest jobs and pay you shit. He promised Juan he would help him get there, start a better life for his family, and he did exactly as he'd promised.

But now...something had changed his cousin. And Juan knew the Chinaman was at fault. The little man had mentioned a special recipe, how powerful it was. How he had used too much of it.

What did you do, you son of a bitch?

Juan helped Manuel to his feet, his cousin's body slick with sweat and the woman's blood. Manuel's eyes were wide, sparkling with desire.

"You take me to the restaurant. Paradise...Buffet." He bit his lip, flared his nostrils. His bloody, red cock began to harden.

Juan led Manuel to the closet, having to step over the mauled body. He tried to avoid stepping on anything, but winced when something soft squashed under his shoe.

"Put some clothes on, and we'll go, okay?"

Manuel nodded. He quickly pulled on a pair of pants, slid into a t-shirt. The blood soaked through the fabric, but it was good enough. Juan didn't know if he could take another eyeful of his cousin biting into the woman, peeling meat away, and he tried to hurry Manuel out the door. But as he wrapped his fist around the doorknob, his other hand in the crook of Manuel's arm, he noticed his cousin's eyes land on the hooker's body. They burned with hunger and savagery.

"Manuel, let's go." Juan tried to pull him along, but Manuel's feet were stapled to the floor.

"I'm so hungry, cousin. My stomach is *killing* me. Just... let me..." He lunged for the girl's body, but Juan held him by the arm. "No! Just one bite...one more *fucking bite!*"

Juan leaned back on his heels and yanked, pulling Manuel into his arms. He wrapped his arm around Manuel's neck and squeezed.

Manuel's hands reached for the body instead of trying to pry the arm away. His teeth clicked. Juan felt warm drool ooze onto his forearm and he cringed, but held tight. "Manuel, stop it! We're going to the buffet. Right now, okay?"

Manuel's struggles halted. His body went limp in Juan's arms, then he spun, his neck slippery with blood, and stood face to face with Juan. His smile nearly split his head in half. "The buffet. Take me there, cousin. We can eat however much we want. The recipe...he changed it."

Juan just nodded and led Manuel out the front door. His cousin chattered the whole way into the parking lot, listing all the different dishes he would eat when they got there.

"Que paso, wey?"

Juan mashed his teeth together and thought they'd crack from the pressure. The troll of the parking lot just wouldn't let up. Juan doubted she even realized she'd been talking to the same guy over and over.

She stepped in front of them and grinned, showing the row of dead flies that were her teeth. "Come on, man. I'll let you both fuck me. Same time, man. Fifty bucks."

Juan tried to ignore her, step around her, but Manuel became cemented where he stood. Juan turned and growled with frustration.

"The hell with your friend, ese." The woman had her

body pressed against Manuel's, her hand fondling the bulge in his pants like she was trying to unscrew a light bulb. "Me and you, baby. Fifteen pesos."

"Muévete a la chingada." Juan shoved her, but Manuel grabbed the back of her head with a cupped hand. He ran his tongue over his teeth, the blood of the dead hooker still thick in his mouth.

"*Mmmm.*"

"That's right, baby. Best pussy you ever had."

Juan tried to stop it, but it felt like he moved in slow motion, like his body had been dipped in glue.

Manuel yanked her hair back, tilting her chin to the sky. She smiled and giggled. The giggles turned to gurgles and chokes as Manuel bit into the middle of her neck. Her skin stretched as he jerked his head away before finally snapping free.

"Manuel…no!" Juan pulled Manuel away from the girl who clawed at her neck as if she could scrape the pain away. Blood splashed at her feet. "We need to go now!"

Manuel grunted as Juan pulled him across the parking lot. "The buffet…*I need it.*"

MIDNIGHT SNACK

Chandra sat in the middle of her living room, covered in blood. She cracked open Fufu's leg bone and sucked the marrow out. Remnants of food packaging littered the house. The refrigerator had fallen and leaned against the kitchen counter. Every bit of food she could find now inhabited her stomach.

But it growled nonetheless.

The pain was like nothing she'd ever known, and she would do anything to calm it. All she could think about was the Paradise Buffet and the succulent saucy meat and deep-fried treats they offered.

It's not far from my house, she thought. *I can just walk there*. The bus didn't run this late, so it was her only choice. Blood coated her pink nightie and bulbous black legs. She tried to roll into a position to stand up, but it proved to be a difficult task, and she held her breath as she rocked herself. Fufu's bones lay in a heap by her side, all broken and strung together with gore.

"My stomach…" Just saying the words was exhausting and she had to take a break to breathe afterward.

It felt like rats chewing their way out of her. She got to her hands and knees, used the couch to get to her feet. Part of her wanted to sit back down and rest, but the demon in her gut urged her to go on.

Chandra knew this wasn't right. She knew something was wrong. There was a small voice in the back of her mind, calling to her, faint as if it were in a cave off in the distance. It was *her* voice. Her real voice. Telling her to stop. Begging her to look at herself, what she was doing, what she had turned into.

But the voice was swallowed whole by her new ravenous

self. All she could think about was her hunger, the pain throbbing in her mid-section.

"Ungh…" She winced as she shuffled her pink slippers across her carpet, the glittery poofs matted with blood and meat and crumbs.

The Paradise Buffet. She didn't know which food she liked best. It didn't matter. Everything they served became one smoldering, mouth-watering dish in her mind. She'd been going there everyday for a week. And ever since that first time, she couldn't stop. It haunted her dreams, her every thought. She could smell the food wherever she was, her mouth salivating in preparation for it.

She'd always been a heavy girl, but since the buffet became her pastime, she nearly doubled in size. But no matter how much she ate, she couldn't satisfy the hunger. It consumed her, it became her. Defined her.

She made it to her front door. It took her a few times to turn the knob since her hands were slick with Fufu fluid, but she got it open, stepped into the night, stared at the moon. It was a water chestnut in the sky and she actually reached for it, clawing at it with pink, bedazzled nails. The stars were sticky rice grains floating in dark sauce.

Her stomach twisted and she groaned as if in labor. She walked into the street, leaving her door open behind her, and headed in the direction of the buffet.

A jogger trotted by, bending his eyebrows at her as he passed.

Chandra reached for him, but missed by a mile. She bared her teeth and waddled after him.

"Crazy bitch," the man said, jogging backward as he spoke. "Ever try a salad?"

"*I'm hungry.*"

"I bet you are." And he turned and disappeared over the horizon.

She wanted to follow him, to flay the flesh from his bones with her teeth, but the buffet called to her. He would only be an appetizer anyway. She turned back around and shambled down the road, in the direction of her food fetish fantasy. The street was a frying pan, the yellow lines strips of bacon. The trees were fried eggrolls, the bushes fried wontons, the grass beef and broccoli. Fatigue began setting in, but her hunger was the mightier beast, and she stormed forward.

She left her neighborhood and reached the busier streets. Cars sped by, the passengers leering out the windows at the blood-covered atrocity stalking down the sidewalk. Some honked their horns, others hollered their revulsion from their windows.

People walking along avoided getting too close, couples pressed tightly together. All wrinkling their noses and curling their lips and furrowing their brows.

"*So hungry...*"

Chandra reached for a woman, got hold of an arm, but it was jerked away. The woman voiced her displeasure, but it was only empty static to Chandra. She swiped at a couple walking hand in hand, wrapped her fingers around the man's swinging wrist, brought it to her mouth, opened wide, but he pulled away just in time, then shoved her away. She stumbled off the curb, rolled into the street, lay there like a beached whale. A station wagon skidded, screeching to a halt just in front of her, just a hair away from splattering her food-filled body across the concrete.

"Jesus. Are you okay?" The driver's head poked out of his window.

Chandra struggled to find her footing. She rolled in the street, just barely aware of the pebbles and sharp rocks biting into her skin.

"Let me help you."

A hand reached out to her, and she reached for the hand, yanked it like a lawnmower chord. The man crashed to the ground beside her and she was on him in a millisecond. Her teeth sunk into the soft flesh. She didn't know what part she bit, but when her mouth filled with flavor and meaty richness, she moaned with pleasure.

"*Shit! Jesus Christ!*" He tried to scurry away, but Chandra rolled and shimmied on top of him.

She ripped mouthfuls of meat away from his body,

swallowed. Screams and shouts blared all around her, and she wept as she ate, knew what she was doing was bad. She knew she had become something...else. But her stomach controlled her now. It sent the brainwaves now. It told her to keep eating, to ignore the pounding of the fists, to ignore the pain-filled groans and whimpers. Other hands found her body, tried to pull her away from her meal. She snapped at them, reaching her head back as far as she could.

She looked down at the meat beneath her, really seeing it for the first time. It was faceless, no longer moving, no longer protesting. A beefy skull stared back at her, its eyes glistening and stained with blood, the sockets swimming pools of crimson. Like meatballs in marinara.

She bent down and sucked them out, squashed them with her molars. Warm jelly flooded her mouth, coated her tongue.

Then she remembered. The Paradise Buffet. That's where she wanted to be. That's where the true delicacies lay. As she rocked herself, trying to find footing, arms and hands attacked from all sides. She was thrown to her back and held there.

"Please, you have to let me go. I have to get to the buffet. I'll die if I don't." She wanted to say this, but all she could muster were moans and labored breaths.

Red and blue lights flashed. Sirens wailed. More shouts.

Chandra looked past the chaos and saw others walking away from her. Big bodies. Balls of lard with arms and legs and mouths, heading in the direction she wanted to be heading.

She couldn't let them get there before her. Had to beat them there. The food belonged to her, and she wouldn't let them have it.

"*Mine!*"

She fought off the restraints of limbs, the people she couldn't see holding her there. Her body wiggled and thrashed. She found a leg and bit into it.

Something struck her chest, vibrated. Like bee stings. She ignored it, bit harder. Screams. Blood rushed past her lips and teeth and down her throat. She climbed the leg, clutched stiff fabric and hauled herself up, finding new strength at the thought of her food being eaten before she could get there. Her stomach twisted.

"They can't have it...buffet is mine..."

More stings, then a blinding liquid in her face. It made her hungrier, reminded her of the General Tso's chicken, the Szechuan beef. Before she knew it, she was on the ground again, her face pressed against the street. Her hands were behind her back, locked there.

"No..."

She tried to move, but found it impossible. Her hunger was at its peak. She turned her head, found her own dark, meaty shoulder. As she began eating it, she wondered if there would be anything left at the Paradise Buffet for her. She hoped the others left her something...anything.

REMAINS

Lola stared at the front of the house, standing just outside of the driveway. The door stood wide open. Stripes of blood tracked from the doorstep down the driveway toward the sidewalk. She had the man's driver's license out, was ready to check the address to make sure she had the right house, but tossed it aside; this was the house.

Do I really want to see what's inside?

The small house reminded her of her father's. Same rusty color, about the same size. She'd spent so many years of her life taking care of him after her mother died, the years when she should have been stressing over school work and boys and acne. Instead, she was elbow deep in Daddy's fat and hairy skin. Bent over his stained sheets. Biting her tongue to keep from screaming. Feeling him shanking her, running his sausage-fingers over her back, her thighs, grunting and growling. Warm sweat trickling down onto her body.

Daddy loves you, honey.

Her radio crackled to life and she jumped in surprise. The frantic voice was chattering about a woman apprehended who'd...eaten someone. Lola's stomach dropped into her socks.

The voice called for backup, mentioned needing EMS for a bite to his leg.

Lola cut the radio off. She felt like she needed silence for some reason. Even though she knew the fat man was dead, that she drilled a bullet straight through him, she felt like he could hear her outside of his house. That he would come stumbling out, chewing on a mouthful of his wife.

Or am I scared that Daddy will come out?

The butterflies in her stomach became yellow jackets as she took quivering steps up the driveway, avoiding the blood, and toward the door.

She could smell her father's bed sores again. *It's all in my head.* She'd always known it was, but it didn't take away from the dread filling her stomach like a clogged sink. Her police-issued .40-calibur Smith and Wesson was back in evidence, but she brought along her own 9 mm.

She was close to positive that she would find a body inside, probably stripped down to the bone. She didn't fully understand why she didn't bring any help along or notify anybody about her plan. Part of her felt she owed the man whose life she took. He wanted someone to check on his wife, and Lola wanted to be that person.

Now that she stood there, in front of that house, blood staining the concrete, she knew it would be a good time to call for backup. Even though she was technically off duty now, she brought her radio just for that reason. The same radio she just cut off.

She was a ten year old girl again. Standing in front of her father's house. The house of her broken childhood. Filled to the brim with bad memories, seeping out through the open door. Sweat trickled down her chest and back.

Come inside, sweetheart. Daddy has a surprise for you. It's right here, under the sheets.

"No. Y-you leave me alone. Don't t-touch me." She caught herself speaking out loud, then shrunk into herself and crumbled onto the driveway. Arms wrapped around knees and she rocked herself, humming a song that she didn't know the title to. She didn't know why she knew the tune, but always sang it to herself when she was afraid. Which meant, as a child, she sang it a lot. *Maybe my mother used to sing it to me,* she thought. *Maybe she used to sing it to me when I was little, when I was scared. To soothe me. To make the monsters go away.*

Festering memories crawled from her subconscious, memories she thought she'd buried beneath an ocean of alcohol, memories she'd beaten flat with endless workouts. She promised herself to never become that frightened little girl again. But they came back like zombies clawing their way up from the center of the Earth.

She stood in the kitchen, cooking. Daddy called from his bedroom. His voice, thick and rattling with phlegm, was accompanied by shouts and moans of pleasure from the adult movies playing on his television. She could even hear the slick sound of his hand, slathered with petroleum jelly, preparing himself.

He told her they were playing pretend. Just like on the movies he watched.

She microwaved a pizza, covered it in hot sauce, just like he liked it. Another plate full of French fries, grease soaking through the paper, topped with mounds of ketchup and melted cheddar cheese. She balanced the plates on one arm, the plate holding the pizza on her forearm, the greasy French fry plate in her hand. The other hand held the mug filled with soda, with five tablespoons of sugar added.

"Hurry up! Daddy's hungry."

"Fuck me," the television screamed.

She entered the room with tears running down her chubby cheeks. The pizza burned her arm, but that pain almost felt good. The room stank of bodily fluids and unwashed skin. Flies buzzed into her face, circled her father like planets orbiting the sun. She had learned to keep her eyes blurred, like looking at a Magic Eye picture, so as not to see the mountain of lard that called itself her father, the beast that ravaged her with no mercy, stuffing food into its stomach as it stole her innocence.

"Come sit down, baby."

"No, no, no, no. *Don't touch me!*" Lola slammed her fists against her head. She felt the cool breeze of the night and realized where she was.

My father is dead. Heart attack. He's not in this house.

She wiped the mucus and tears from her face and took shuddering breaths. The pain in her knuckles called her attention and she saw the shredded skin and blood from where she was grinding them into the cement. Her gun lay beside her like a dead bird.

The fear started to creep back into her mind, and she slammed her fist into the driveway. The pain was good, drove the fear back to her stomach. She hit it again, and again.

"Fuck you!" Her fist cracked against the pavement. One of the bones in her hand snapped and bent the skin like a tent. But it felt damn good. She tried to squeeze a fist, couldn't, winced from the burn, but got to her feet. Her injured hand hung at her side, and she bent down and plucked the gun with her other hand—the trigger-pulling hand. She squeezed the metal in her palm and marched the rest of the way to the front door.

The air was electric with violent energy. It ran across her skin and burrowed deep into her viscera. She stalked through the house, following the streaks of blood until she came to the kitchen.

The text book signs of a struggle: overturned table and chairs, various items disheveled and tossed about.

And then she found her.

Lola's injured hand floated up and covered her mouth as she peered at the kitchen floor. The woman lay motionless, just as she'd suspected, in a pool of blood that stretched out and touched the walls on either side of her. Her entire left arm had been stripped down to the bone, tiny bits of meat and sinew here and there. The hand was intact though, looked like a glove, and the gold wedding ring shone in the fluorescent light.

Lola bent down, shaking her head. Her eyes rolled across the bloodied body until reaching the woman's face. A cheek was gone, torn away to reveal the muscle fibers and teeth beneath.

Lola reached out with her good hand, brushed the woman's hair out of her face.

"I'm so sorry."

When the woman's eye popped open, Lola screamed and fell backward. She tried to catch herself, but the pain in her hand exploded and she toppled over. Her other hand instinctively went for her gun, but she caught herself and crawled toward the woman instead.

Through the ragged ripped flesh on the woman's face, her teeth moved up and down, clicking together as she gasped for air. She choked and spat up blood. Her breaths whistled and a faint, rattling moan seeped from her throat; her body shuddered, but she didn't move. Except her eye, bloodshot and covered with burst blood vessels. It landed on Lola and stayed there for what seemed like a lifetime.

"B...b..."

Lola laid a gentle hand on the woman's head. "We'll get you some help. Just stay quiet." She snapped her radio on, gave the address, and requested an ambulance.

"Buf...buffet." She went into a coughing fit that sprayed an inkblot of blood onto the cabinet door beside her.

"What did you say?" Lola knew exactly what she was trying to say. It was something she'd known since picking up this woman's husband from that restaurant.

The woman whimpered, let out a sigh, and lay still. Her eye rolled slightly and landed on the ceiling just past Lola's face.

Help was coming. The dispatcher's voice squawking from her radio, begging her for more information, was only background noise to her. She cut it off.

The Paradise Buffet. She pictured the restaurant full of morbidly obese creatures, skin bags of calories, just stuffing themselves to the point of ripping open and spilling out. Pictured her father in his bed, killing himself more and more every day, eating and eating until he couldn't fit out of his bedroom door.

She imagined her town full of zombie-like, insatiable mounds of lard, lumbering through the streets, eating anything in their path.

It was like Daddy had escaped her nightmares and possessed them all. Spread his seed in the food and was transforming everyone into versions of himself.

Lola was in her own personal Hell.

The streets would run yellow with fat.

Chubby fingers reaching, grabbing. Teeth gnashing, grinding.

Lola stood and ran out of the house. With her gun in hand, she made for the restaurant.

And all the while, Daddy cackled inside of her head.

95

DESCENT

The parking lot light poles shone cones of yellow down onto the black, cracked concrete. The white stripes that blocked off individual parking spots were faded and barely distinguishable. Bugs danced and fluttered with the warmth of the light, powerless to resist the call of it. They slapped against the bulb, some plummeted down to the ground only to rise again and head right back to the glorious brightness.

But they were not the only ones attracted by a force that called to them on some deeper level, so deep that they became shells of their former selves, mindlessly wandering toward their destination.

They ignored each other for the most part. Some looked up in confusion as other plump bodies bumped into them or passed them by. There were looks of jealousy and greed traded amongst them, as if whoever got there first would get it all.

The food.

It's what they all wanted—what they needed—a desire more powerful than love or survival.

Their stomachs roared and boiled and brought some of them to their knees, grimacing and howling. But they would not be denied. They would find their will to go on again, especially when others rushed past them, heading toward the glass front of the Paradise Buffet.

So many of them now. Every one of them wrapped tightly in clothing that may have once fit. Now, after weeks of over-indulgence of the specially prepared Chinese food, with the brand new recipe the Asian man bragged about, fat bulged out of sleeves and collars and sandals. He was right, of course. The food was incredible. More addicting than crack or meth or sex or gambling.

96

An elderly woman clutched her stomach and whimpered as she fell forward and cracked her face on the hard parking lot. A couple of teeth rattled loose, but she took no notice of the pain. That pain was but a flutter compared to that in her belly, burning her like she'd swallowed sulfuric acid. Blood ran from the craters in her spotted, pink gums. She lapped it up as she tried to stand.

A group of teenagers wearing letterman jackets that looked on the verge of breaking at the seams trudged forward as a unit, knocking others to the side. They elbowed at each other as they went, all trying to bully their way to the front of the pack. One of them trampled over the older woman. His knee collided with the back of her head, sending her back to the ground, her face hurtling back to the cement. He stepped on the back of her head, grinding her in, but took no notice.

The woman, her face a mess of red and black, stood up and continued toward the restaurant. Her church dress had torn down the front, revealing her dried out flesh beneath, but she could only think of one thing. And it lay beyond those glass doors.

More and more came—all the same. They chanted, not as one, but every one of them voiced their desires.

"Food."

"So...hungry."

"My stomach. Need to eat..."

"Buffet... I need the buffet."

They gathered at the doors, pushing and shoving and pressing into each other. Fat mashed together, forming one, flailing tsunami of lard and thrashing limbs and drooling mouths and wide eyes.

The glass bent from the pressure of them all. The restaurant was dark, but they could see the gleaming stainless steel of the buffet.

A man, crushed from all sides, whimpered from the pain in his mid-section. His lip quivered and he searched for a way to the front, viciously desperate to put out the raging fire in his belly with piles of saucy meat. He bared his teeth, tried to move, but couldn't. The boy next to him did the same.

The man, unable to move anything but his head, leaned over and clamped his teeth over the boy's meaty shoulder. His mouth flooded with warmth and his stomach thanked him as he swallowed. The pain dulled, but only for a moment. So he went for another bite. He noticed that the boy was chewing on *his* fatty side, ripping the skin open and gorging on the soft fat, but he did nothing to stop it. There was another sting from behind, from his other side, somewhere by his leg. But none of that mattered. He took another considerable chunk from the boy's arm and let the meat melt over his tongue.

The crowd pulsated as it began to eat itself.

The mass of bodies bulged and grew tighter as more joined from the streets. The cries of pain and hunger became a rumbling of wet sound. Their rattling, labored breathing merged together into one terrible, chaotic symphony.

Blood and chunks of ragged meat hit the ground and stained their shins and shoes. They begged for the food, but took what they could get.

Each other.

The glass warped and a spider web of cracks began spreading across it.

FEAST

Juan struggled to get the key into the lock at the back door of the restaurant. He avoided the front because he wasn't sure if Mr. Chan was still there or not. Sure, he wanted to give the son of a bitch a piece of his mind, fantasizing about getting some form of sweet revenge for ruining his cousin, but right at that moment, he wanted to get in and out as quietly as possible.

He couldn't believe he was back in the fucking restaurant. After witnessing his cousin gorging himself on human flesh, all he wanted was to be home, with his family, away from this living nightmare.

But Manuel needed him. Manuel was losing control of himself and would hurt others, possibly get himself killed if left unattended. And the only thing that calmed him was the promise of Mr. Chan's food. He ground his teeth and smacked his lips behind Juan, the Mexican girl's blood tingeing his skin.

So there he was, using the key he'd just obtained hours earlier to break into the restaurant and feed his cousin. Manuel shook with anticipation as they entered the kitchen.

"General Tso's chicken. That's what I want first. A big bowl of that. Then beef and broccoli. Okay, cousin? And then..."

"Quiet, Manuel. We'll get you the food, but we need to stay quiet."

Manuel grabbed his stomach and his face twisted with pain. "Then...I want eggrolls, a mountain of eggrolls. And a bowl of pork lo mein. And fried rice. Yeah...*ungh.*"

Juan winced with every sound. This was hopeless. He could only pray that Mr. Chan wasn't there, that they could get Manuel fed and get the hell out as soon as possible.

They walked out of the alleyway and into the black hole of the kitchen. Juan took slow, steady steps as he went, trying not to bump anything. Sharp angles and gleaming metal started to take shape as his eyes adjusted to the darkness. He stopped and spun his head from left to right, Manuel's gasping breaths huffing behind him, quick and shallow like he was masturbating back there.

Juan thought he saw movement through the little plastic window on the double doors that led to the dining room, but he wasn't sure. He stared at it, squinted. Manuel grabbed his shoulders from behind and breathed hot, fetid air into the back of his neck. Juan jerked away, afraid of being bitten. The image of Manuel's teeth ripping away chunks of hooker meat was fresh in his mind.

Half of a scream escaped his throat, but he slapped his hand over his mouth and swallowed the rest of the sound.

Manuel's eyes and lips sparkled in the darkness. "The cooler. The food...it's there." He pointed to the other side of the kitchen, rubbed his stomach with the other hand.

"Okay, stay here. Let me get you something." Juan's plan was to grab what he could and escape as quickly as possible. He would use the rest of his pay to get them a hotel somewhere. A room with a kitchen so he could cook this fucking food. Keep his cannibalistic cousin subdued for as long as it took for him to figure out their next step.

Two American girls dead. Eaten.

The only thing he could think of was to get them back home. To Mexico. Neither of them had any papers, no way for the cops to find out who they were. They were just a couple of faceless, cockroach wetbacks, and Juan was actually glad about that. One and a half days in the United States, and everything went to shit. Juan went through hell to get there, now he would have to find a way out. Part of him felt frustrated with the idea of it, but the other part, the bigger part, was glad to go home. To be with his family. The hell with it all.

Juan rushed for the cooler door, swung it open. A light clicked on and illuminated the over-stocked room. Cardboard boxes stacked higher than his head in all directions, all with indecipherable Chinese lettering. His breaths were clouds of vapor. The sweat that had formed across his body chilled and sent shivers past his bones and into his marrow.

Manuel shoved past him. He circled in place and his eyes became perfect circles. His skin was dyed red, some of the blood flaking off from his neck as he turned his head from side to side. A glob of saliva drooped from his mouth and puddled between his feet.

"My...stomach. It needs it, cousin. I have to...eat. Eat it all up."

Juan reached for Manuel's shoulder, but his cousin bared his teeth and snapped at the hand. Juan backed away, shaking his head.

Can I help him? Is it too late?

Manuel yanked at boxes and plastic packaging and brought them crashing to the ground. Raw chicken breasts, beef shoulder roasts, pork tenderloin. Packages of spices and bread crumbs and sauces. It all rained down on him and he grabbed whatever his fingers could wrap around first and gorged. He moaned erotically as his mouth was filled and food slid down his throat.

Juan held his hand over his mouth. The familiar tang of acid coated the back of his throat as he watched. Manuel swallowed chicken breasts whole, biting down on the meat to go through the motions rather than to actually chew the food. His throat bulged like a snake swallowing a rat, and Manuel would choke and make a clicking sound until finally getting it down. He never slowed. His hands slammed food into his face faster than he could swallow.

Juan turned to escape watching it any more, and found himself looking into the barrel of a pistol. Behind it, Mr. Chan stared at him with narrowed eyes.

SEA OF FAT

Lola's car nearly rolled over as she slammed her foot against the brake pedal. It skidded across the parking lot and barely missed smashing into one of the light poles.

Then she saw them.

Jesus Christ.

Panic rose from her stomach and into her throat. A scream wanted to escape, but she breathed through it. Just the sight of so many bulbous bodies, so many rolls of fat, threatened to take hold of her sanity and squeeze it until it crumbled away.

She couldn't help it. No matter how hard she tried to stop it, she was powerless. Every one of them became her father.

They looked like oil in a deep fryer, bubbling and wriggling and undulating in front of the glass. Arms flailed, fingers groped. Sweat gleamed and sparkled from jiggling skin. From where Lola sat, she could see them biting into each other, chewing and licking. Blood caked the ground beneath them. Even with her windows rolled up, she heard them. She heard the congregation of Daddies sucking and groaning and grunting. From inside of her head, she could hear him calling her, begging her to join, to be with him again. To let him take her into his body like she had done with him, over and over and over. He wanted her inside of *him* now.

Lola! Come to us, baby. Let our teeth and fingers pull you apart. Let Daddy taste you.

Moisture leaked from her hands and made the steering wheel slick. She banged her forehead against it, letting the pain calm her. Her hand throbbed as she tried to clench it.

"Leave me a-alone. You're dead. I'm glad you're dead."

I'm right here.

She wondered why her mother didn't speak to her. Why she didn't do something to help her. If her father had the power to torture her from beyond the grave, then surely she could to.

"Where the fuck are you? Help me!"

There was no soothing voice. There was no song.

But Daddy was there, just like he always was.

Mama is gone. She's in my tummy. Aaalll gone.

Lola scooped up the gun from the passenger seat and peered through the windshield toward the roiling bodies. She blinked her eyes, shook her head, slammed the metal of the gun against her scalp. But when she looked, she still saw Daddy. Every face, every mouth, every stomach. They were him.

And she wanted to shoot every fucking one of them. She wanted to see blood and fat pour from the bullet holes, mixing together into an orange sludge as it rushed out of them. Craved to see them collapse motionless to the ground, just like the man at the station.

I'll kill them all.

She stepped out of the car, eased the door shut. The glass front of the restaurant warped and bended inward, and cracks spread across the surface. It wouldn't be long before it exploded from the weight. Any second.

Even as they feasted on each other, it was the food from the buffet they wanted; she knew that now. She remembered how they looked when she was apprehending the fat man. How they ignored everything, even their own pain, as they stuffed their faces.

It was the Chinaman. Even Jennings mentioned how terrible the food used to be there. But the little Asian man changed the recipe. He did something to it, added something to create this mutant craving.

He was the reason for the gang of Daddies submerging Lola into this nightmare, drowning her in lard. And she would get *him* too.

She stalked across the vast stretch of concrete, leaving her vehicle running behind her. Her gun held tightly in her grasp, the other hand gripping the pulsing pain.

Will my fellow officers be showing up on scene any time soon? She hoped not. Wanted these fuckers all to herself. And she wasn't in the mood to follow procedure...or to arrest anyone. She wanted to stop hearts. She wanted to turn them into Swiss cheese.

She wanted Daddy's voice to go away.

Her eyes burned with vengeance as she neared the horde of corpulence. She could smell them. Like greasy bed sores seeping poisonous juice. Their sound sent quivers over her skin and caused her eye to twitch.

Then, like being hit by a charging rhinoceros, Daddy smashed into her from her blind spot. He straddled her and grinned like the Devil.

SLOP IN THE TROUGH

Mr. Chan looked past Juan and into the cooler. Juan expected him to lose it, to shout about how they were stealing, how he would call the police. But his face went slack and the hard, take-no-shit look blurred into a droop of worry. He pointed the gun at Manuel and moved Juan aside with his bandaged hand.

"They all the same. Like monsters." The gun shook as he aimed it. Juan saw tears strolling down his bony cheeks.

"Manuel sick. What you do to him?" Juan's eyes ping-ponged from the gun to Mr. Chan's face. He thought about going for it, but not yet.

"I did it. It my fault. They...they everywhere." The gun stayed trained on Manuel, but Mr. Chan looked at Juan. "Outside. They want in."

"¿Quien?"

"My grandfather's recipe...he tell me not to use too much. I no listen. I want successful business. I want...I want my wife back."

Juan cocked his head and listened, could hear them in the distance. The shouts and moans. The pounding of flesh against glass. He knew what was out there: the customers of the restaurant, the eaters. All just like Manuel. All hungry. All trying to get inside.

The back door.

He'd left it open, hoping to get out fast. Juan turned toward it, made a dash for it, but it swung in just as he reached for it and the edge caught him in the forehead. He slammed backward into the counter, then fell to the floor. Blood trickled down his face and blinded him, giving everything a red hue.

The staff. They shoved each other to get inside, all of

them bleeding from bite wounds decorating their bodies like polka dots, soaking through their clothing. The dishwasher entered first, snarling and clutching at his stomach.

Mr. Chan fired.

Juan flinched from the sound, scooted backward across the floor, and tried to hide himself behind a trashcan. He wiped at the blood on his face, winced as his head throbbed. His ears rang from the blast that lingered and bounced off the metal countertops.

The back of the dishwasher's head had a ragged hole the size of a baseball. He fell to his knees, then forward onto his face. The blood spread with quickness.

The others didn't even notice. They trampled the body and pushed toward the cooler. They didn't even care that Mr. Chan had his gun ready, pointing the smoking barrel right at them.

He fired again. And again. He unloaded the pistol until it clicked empty.

Two more bodies fell, their eyes open and sightless. One of them, that Juan recognized as Consuelo, jerked and spasmed on the floor. His lower jaw moved up and down as if chewing on an invisible cut of meat.

"Stay back," Mr. Chan said. He kept pulling the trigger, hoping for magic bullets. Then he finally threw the gun and looked toward Juan. "Help me."

Juan said nothing. The remaining three Mexicans stepped over their fallen comrades and went straight for the cooler. They could care less about Mr. Chan when what they craved so violently was only a few steps away.

But Manuel saw them coming. And he was in no mood to share.

Juan tried to grab the cooler door as it slammed shut. He knew if they couldn't get inside, that him and Mr. Chan would start to look a lot like dinner.

His fingers almost caught it, but they slipped off and the door slammed shut. He heard a commotion coming from inside and imagined Manuel using something to barricade the door.

The former employees ran their fingers over the door,

moaned and clutched their stomachs. They tried the handle, but the door wouldn't budge. Without a moment's pause, they turned and found Mr. Chan. Two of the three went for him, clicking their teeth and letting their tongues hang out like panting dogs. Mr. Chan shouted Chinese at them, frantically searched the kitchen for something to defend himself with. He found a serrated butcher knife lying on the counter, wrapped his fingers around its hilt.

But Juan didn't have a chance to see what happened.

The third Mexican, Juan recognized as the man who delivered the prepared food to the buffet, came at him. His eyes wild, the color of blood, quivering and pained. The man bared his teeth, the silver caps within glinting like buried treasure.

Juan sent the sole of his shoe upward and caught the man on the bottom of the chin. A spray of blood misted into the air, but the man wasn't slowed.

Juan searched for some kind of weapon, anything. From where he sat, he saw nothing that looked useful. He sent another kick toward the man as the attacker fell to his knees and descended on Juan, but it bounced off of his chest harmlessly.

The man caught Juan's foot this time, pulled him close with a powerful tug. The joint popped at his groin and Juan hissed. Then screamed when the teeth clamped onto his calf. Even with his jeans in the way, the teeth pinched the meat of his leg.

There was a box beneath the counter just beside him. He grabbed for it, got hold of it, and threw it at the man. It was weightless, did no damage. But an explosion of fortune cookies showered out like cellophane fireworks.

"C-comida." The man released Juan's leg and went for the plastic-wrapped cookies. He stuffed them into his mouth without opening them, the plastic crinkling as he chewed.

Juan jumped to his feet...and saw Mr. Chan. He hadn't noticed what was going on as he fought for his own life, didn't hear the gurgling cries of pain, the wet sounds of chewing.

The two Mexicans had him pinned to the ground like lions on a gazelle. One tore strips of muscle from the arm, licking the bone underneath. The other, with the knife protruding from his chest, rolled his face over the Chinaman's throat and groaned. Blood poured onto the floor as Mr. Chan's mouth worked up and down, his eyes searching the ceiling, drowning in tears.

Juan thought about making a run for the door, escaping the pandemonium, but he just couldn't leave his cousin behind. There was no way he would end up a meal for these sons of bitches, though. He wouldn't let them have him.

He dashed across the kitchen. His shoes slid on Mr. Chan's blood and nearly made him slip, but he kept his balance as he reached the first man. One hand took a fistful of hair as the other wrenched the knife free from the man's chest. Juan yanked the hair backward, clenched his teeth, and sawed the man's neck open. The serrated edge of the knife ate into the flesh with ease, breaking open the skin and releasing a fountain of blood. Juan ran the blade back and forth, pressing down until he felt bone.

The man spat, coughed, and gurgled, but still swallowed the mouthful of Mr. Chan's neck meat that he'd been chewing. Red chunks slid out from the open mess on his own neck and he fell over, motionless. The other man didn't even flinch and continued his feast of the arm, but Juan did him the same way, nearly decapitating him. He let his body drop on top of Mr. Chan's.

"T-tengo...hambre..."

The last one left, having finished the fortune cookies, was back on his feet. He reached for Juan and took rapid breaths, inflating and deflating his stomach.

"¡Ir al Infierno!" Juan held the knife in front of him as he ran forward like a raging bull. The blade sunk to the hilt, just over the man's heart. Juan's momentum, fueled by a massive dose of adrenaline, caused him to tumble when they collided, and they both crashed to the floor, Juan on top. The hilt of the knife jabbed him in the chest when he fell on it. There was a crack, and a jolt of pain speared through him. He rolled onto his back and kicked his legs as he struggled to breathe.

The man wiggled a bit beside him, his tongue thrashing from between his lips, then he went still. His head went limp and fell to the side, his eyes landing on Juan's as a trickle of blood ran from the corner of his mouth.

Juan clambered to his knees. Every movement sent a stabbing pain through his chest. He touched where the hilt had jabbed him, grimaced. Broken rib. Maybe two.

"M...my...f-fault."

Juan crawled toward Mr. Chan, and with a considerable amount of pain, rolled the leaking body of the worker whose head dangled by the spine off of him.

Mr. Chan took whistling breaths through the wreckage of his throat. Juan couldn't tell how, but somehow the man could speak. Barely audible and covered in wet, sticky sounds, but he struggled to say more.

"Out...s-side. M-more...more of them. We...all...d-dead."

Just as Mr. Chan's face went limp and the last whistling breath sang from his neck, Juan heard the explosion of glass breaking.

PINNED

Lola pounded her fists against the soft, squishy body, ignoring the searing pain in her injured hand. Her legs kicked, her head rolled. But the body was too heavy. It poured over her as she was pinned to the concrete by its weight. She screamed, then growled and peered at Daddy as he smiled down at her and licked his lips.

"Hey, girl." Jennings winced and bared his teeth. "My fucking stomach...I gotta eat something." His fingertips ran down her cheek. "But there ain't nothing wrong with eating your dessert first, right?"

Daddy's face rearranged and she saw that it was her partner. Sweat dripped from his forehead and sprinkled onto her face. He smelled of armpits and cheap cologne.

Glass shattered to their right. The moans and whimpers of the crowd became shouts of excitement as they poured into the restaurant. Jennings twisted his head and watched them. Lola felt him twitch, as if he desperately wanted to join them. His eyelids trembled, his brow furrowed. His stomach rumbled.

But his head turned back down at Lola. She felt something stiff prodding her on the hip and she struggled harder than ever to get out from under the mountain of fat, but it was useless.

"Let me go, you fucking pig."

Drool stretched from his lip and slithered over her neck. She felt it run down the creases. Then menacing pain as Jennings bent down and bit into her.

His head jerked and she felt the flesh rip. He was face to face with her again, chewing on a piece of her, fluttering his eyes. Blood ran down his chin, sprinkled her face.

The side of her neck throbbed and stung as the wind hit

110

it. Warmth ran out of her as she took gasping breaths.

Jennings swallowed. "Mmmm, you're...delicious." He ground his hips and poked her with his iron cock. The hand that had been holding her wrist to the ground moved to her chest and kneaded her breast. Her shirt was ripped free and the cool air almost felt good, soothing. Then she felt his slimy tongue sliding across her flesh, his teeth biting down on her nipple. Soft at first, almost playfully, then hard. He groaned and chewed the dark flesh—his body shuddered.

Lola saw Daddy again. His glistening, spotted skin. His sunken, hungry eyes. Her hand went to her chest, came away covered in blood. Fingers hardened into claws and she reached up and raked them across his face. Red, jagged lines were drawn on his skin, but he only breathed harder. A smile pulled the corners of his mouth.

Open up for Daddy.

"N-no!" She jammed her thumb into his left eye, pushed until she felt it pop.

That got some attention. He rolled away and clutched his face, but only for an instant. The jelly that ran down his cheek was met by his tongue and he slurped it up. Then bared his teeth at Lola.

She turned her head, searched the ground for her gun. It had been in her hand when she left her car.

More pain. The skin above her collar bone tore free and Jennings let it hang from his mouth. As he chewed, he reached down, pulled her pants to the middle of her thighs.

"No...*no!*" She thrust her fist and caught him in the nose, felt it crack under her knuckles.

But he had her pants lower, almost to the knees now. He went for his zipper.

Lola spun her head, nearly shouted when she saw the black metal of the pistol just above her head. She reached for it...just out of reach.

Yes, baby. Daddy loves you.

Something hot and hard poked her, tried to invade her.

Spinning her head back toward Jennings, she screamed until the wound in her neck felt like it had torn wider. A growl crackled from her throat as she sat up and bit into him. She didn't know what she bit, but her mouth filled with sweaty, squishy flesh. Her weight took her back to the ground, and the meat tore away. The back of her skull cracked against the pavement, sending sparks of light dancing in her peripherals. Coppery liquid and jelly-like meat filled her mouth, but the stream of vomit that rushed from her stomach pushed it out.

Blood poured from Jennings's throat. His weight lifted, just slightly.

Lola scooted herself backward, reached for the gun, almost knocked it further away with her knuckles. Her fingers wrapped around the handle and she swung around, pressed the barrel into the ragged hole of his neck.

The force of the shots tossed his body back, but his lower half still had her pinned. He bent backward and hung there and Lola dug her heels and palms into the concrete, pulling and straining until it felt like her eyes would burst from the pressure.

She freed herself from the bulk of her former partner, rolled onto her stomach and wept. Every jerking sob sent shivers of pain through her body and she felt herself getting cold, weaker.

She got to her knees, wobbled in place for a moment, then pushed herself to her feet and looked toward the restaurant.

What used to be the windowed front was a mess of broken glass and blood. The jiggling horde had disappeared into the darkness of the Paradise Buffet.

Lola squeezed the handle of her pistol and spat a wad of thick blood to the black ground. She began stalking across the parking lot, ready to end the night, end everything.

Come and get some, sweetheart.

She stopped, turned, growled. Her feet stomped across the blacktop until she reached Jennings's—Daddy's—bent, blubbery corpse. The swollen head of his cock poked through the teeth of his zipper.

"Fuck you."

Lola pointed her gun and emptied it.

POURING IN

The restaurant filled with the moans and grunts of the pigs it fed. Juan scrambled across the kitchen floor, his hands shaking and bloody. He went for the cooler door, banged on it.

"Manuel! We have to go. Now!" He slapped his palms against the stainless steel, kicked at it. His calf burned and blood trickled into his shoe, oozing between his toes. He pulled on the handle, and the door shifted, but wouldn't open. Something in his chest popped and Juan yelped and clutched it. Every breath was painful. His eye instantly dried out from the cold air that seeped out of the cooler as he peered into it through the crack in the door.

Manuel sat on the floor, breaking open another box of meat. He pulled out a whole pork tenderloin and dangled it over his face like a dead snake. Pink juice dripped down and Manuel opened his mouth to take it in.

"Open the door." Juan didn't know if being inside of the cooler would be any better than staying outside with the others, but he would take his chances. If his cousin didn't hurry, Juan would have to leave him there. Manuel was his best friend, had been since they were children, but he had his family to worry about. He couldn't die, they needed him.

Manuel turned and smiled at Juan. "So good, cousin. But it's mine." He let half of the tenderloin slide down his throat, looked like a sword swallower.

Manuel had propped a thick mop handle through the door handle from inside, had it wedged against the wall. Juan pulled on the door, felt it give just a little more, heard the crack of wood.

The footsteps thundered from the dining room. He knew the fat pigs were scavenging out there, hoping to find something, anything. But there was nothing out there.

113

And just then, the double doors swung in. A boy, no older than seventeen, followed by three others just like him, stumbled in. They clawed at their stomachs and whimpered when they saw Juan. The boys were shoved forward as more came. And more.

Ay Dios mío.

Wide faces, open mouths. Their eyes darted around the room, tongues slithering across their lips and teeth. Women and men and children and seniors. Their bodies jiggled as they bumped into each other, clogging the doorway like cholesterol blocking an artery. They all had blood staining their faces, all had bite marks and chunks of flesh missing here and there.

Two children, red-headed boys, their freckled skin bulging from under their clothing, ran across the room and attacked the bodies. One scooped the brains from the back of the dishwasher's head, licked his fingers clean. The other went for Mr. Chan, slurping at the wound on his neck.

It was all the others needed.

"Hungry!"

"It's…it's mine!"

The eaters poured in and Juan backed away from the cooler door. He fell backward and cracked his tailbone on the floor, winced and clutched his chest, then scooted toward the knife that stuck out of the corpse's chest. He wrapped his fingers around the metal handle and tugged. The man's body jerked with it, but the blade stayed hidden in flesh.

A portly woman fell to her knees beside the body, bit into the man's face like she was giving him CPR. She pulled his lips off with her teeth and chewed on them like bubble gum.

A man and woman jumped on the corpse next. Juan still had his hand on the knife handle, then grabbed it with his other hand. As he gave it another tug, the fat trio pulled in the opposite direction and the knife popped free.

Juan jumped to his feet and held the knife in front of him, watching as the kitchen continued to fill with hogs. They fought for the bodies like starved wolves, snapping at each other.

"Give me…food." An old woman, her face stained black and bleeding, stepped toward Juan. A pruney breast swung from her chest through the torn front of her dress. Mounds of wrinkled flesh poured over each other from her midsection.

"Q-quedarse atrás." Juan swiped the knife through the air, but she didn't notice it.

Fat bulged from her shoes as she stepped toward him, her mouth oozing bloody drool. She cried out, nearly crumpled over as her stomach growled with fury. Then she came at him.

His knife went into her mouth and stuck into the back of her throat. She sprayed blood into his face along with a gust of hot, rank air. Her jaw moved up and down, driving the blade of the knife between her teeth and slicing into her gums. Then she fell.

And they were on her in an instant. Grabbing hold of the loose, fatty skin and tearing it away. Her entrails slid out and steamed in the cool air.

Then, Juan heard gunshots.

TAKE THAT

The glass crunched under her shoes as she entered the restaurant and snapped a new magazine into the pistol. A bald-headed man in a football jersey and jeans sat on the soaking rug. The fish tank's contents lay on the floor around him and the golden tail of a coy thrashed from between his lips.

He looked up at Lola as he gnashed his teeth into the scaly fish.

Lola pointed and fired.

She coughed and blood dribbled from her mouth. Her broken hand was pressed over the wound on her neck, but no matter how much pressure she put there, the blood kept pumping. Walking became more difficult by the second. The restaurant blurred and started to go black, but she pushed on.

There was a commotion coming from across the room and she moved toward it. She stumbled into a table, nearly fell over, but steadied herself.

It came from the kitchen. The fat fucks were shoving through the kitchen door, and even with it being double wide, they couldn't fit. One of the stragglers in the back, a teenage girl with white-headed acne littering her face, turned and saw Lola. She chewed on something red, and her silver braces shone through it.

"Mmmm."

As Lola moved closer, she saw that the girl chewed on a chunk of meat bitten off the man beside her. Blood oozed from the hole in his shoulder, but he only shoved at the other bodies blocking his way into the kitchen. Then he bit into a mound of flesh belonging to one of the undulating piles of fat in front of him.

They all did. As they thrashed and fought with each

116

other, they feasted. Bit into the closest body and chewed on the fatty meat.

The girl licked her lips and stumbled toward Lola.

Lola aimed and pulled the trigger.

The girl's head kicked back, and she crumbled to the floor.

Come closer, baby. Let Daddy see your pretty face.

Lola's knees wobbled and she side stepped as she almost lost consciousness. She squinted toward the crowd, saw blurred vibrations.

They were her father. All of them. And they had to die.

She curled her lips back, widened her eyes, went straight for them. Her gun barrel was pressed to the back of a man's skull, then spat a bullet into it. The woman next to him caught the next bullet. Both of their bodies dropped like sacks of jelly.

This was repeated again and again, but her vision swam and she became disoriented as she continued pulled the trigger. She just aimed toward the crowd and fired, then fell backward when her legs gave out.

Such a pretty girl. Let Daddy see how pretty you are.

"You son of a bitch…" Lola clenched her teeth and forced herself back up. She grabbed the edge of a table and held it tight as she rose shakily to her feet.

She ran her forearm over her eyes but couldn't wipe away the blurriness. A pile of bodies lay in front of the kitchen doors, speckled with bullet holes.

The kitchen doors swung closed, rocking and slapping against the bodies. However many were left, they were in the kitchen now. Probably eating every piece of Paradise Buffet they could grab with their chubby fingers.

Lola checked her gun. Magazine empty. One left in the chamber.

She had a good idea what she'd do with that.

Daddy's waiting for you, honey.

CORNERED

Juan inched along the wall and got back to the cooler. He peeked through the crack and watched as Manuel continued to gorge himself. Manuel's stomach looked on the verge of tearing, bulging out from under his shirt.

"Manuel. Open the door."

"I can't...they can't have it. You can't have it." He shook his head as he spoke and bits of chewed food fell out in clumps. It was as if he'd run out of room. But that didn't stop him from trying. He bit into a beef shoulder, snorted as he tried to swallow it.

Juan's mustache twitched and he slammed his fist into the door, then cried out at the stabbing pain in his chest.

Someone was in the dining area with a gun, and Juan didn't want to wait around to find out who it was. This was it. Manuel was on his own.

Juan gave the door one more tug, but it held fast. "I'm sorry, cousin."

A pair of hands grabbed hold of Juan's shoulders, and without hesitation, he spun and swung the knife.

A woman, her face caked with makeup, took the impact to the side of the face. The blade sunk into her flabby cheek and scraped against bone. Juan pulled the knife back out with a slurp, then lodged it under her chin. It pushed through the layers of chins and stabbed into the roof of her mouth. The blade propped her mouth open and blood poured out as she tried to move her jaw.

Juan let go of the knife and juked around her, trying to get to the back door. The bodies of the Mexican workers lay there, along with Mr. Chan...or what was left of them. The eaters still worked at them, tugging on entrails and flaying muscle and tendon away from bone.

Juan looked toward the double doors. The path looked clear, but he didn't know what lay beyond them. Just as he started toward them, a woman burst through the doors... the cop. The pretty police officer from before. She looked pale as she staggered into the kitchen, stepping over a hill of bloated corpses.

She had one hand on her neck, blood seeping from between her fingers. Another ragged wound had opened her chest and the exposed muscle glistened. The other hand held the gun which hung at her side, her arm shaking so hard that the gun knocked against her knee.

A mouthful of blood burst from her lips as she coughed, almost toppled over. Juan ran toward her but slid to a stop when the gun rose from her side and stared at his chest.

"S-stay away. You can't t-touch me anymore..." She fell to her knees and used the gun to steady herself, the barrel pressed against the floor.

Juan sprinted to her side, draped her arm over his neck. "I help you."

A group of four eaters had their eyes on Juan and the woman. They stalked across the kitchen and clicked their teeth. Blood covered them from head to stomach.

"So...*hungry.*"

"I won't l-let you touch me...again," the woman whispered. The gun slipped from her fingers and clattered to the floor. Her body went slack and she became dead weight in Juan's arms.

Her body dropped to the ground, and Juan bent down and scooped up the pistol. He'd never used one before, but he only needed one bullet. He hoped there *was* one.

The group of eaters descended upon the woman and Juan quickly looked away. He ran to the cooler door, gave it one hard tug. He peered into the crack, saw Manuel motionless on the floor. Chewed up meat lay all around him.

He pressed the gun to the thick shaft of wood, pulled the trigger. It went off and Juan fell backward, the gun sliding out of sight.

And he felt the cool air hit his skin.

The rest of them knew what it was. It sounded like stampeding elephants as they stomped toward the cooler. They piled into it, grabbing everything they saw, swallowing chunks of meat whole.

Every one of them pressed into the refrigerator, barely fitting as they fed on the contents. The secret recipe of the Paradise Buffet. Like a bright light for junebugs.

When the last jiggling body crammed into the cooler, Juan slammed the door shut, but it bounced back out when it hit the spongy wall of bodies. He pressed his body against the door, but couldn't quite get it shut.

"L-let 'em...eat each other...to d-death." The woman bared her teeth and leaned into the door as Juan did the same. Bite marks decorated her arms and face.

Together they pushed, grunting and groaning, until finally, the door clicked shut.

The woman fell to the floor, a slight smile on her face, and moved no more.

Juan grabbed everything he could manage to move on his own: shelves, tables, boxes. He shoved them and piled them against the door, though he knew the fat sons of bitches inside wouldn't have the room to turn, much less get that door open.

He thought about Manuel. Probably a greasy spot under the horde's feet by now. He would shed many tears for his cousin...but that would have to come later.

He had to get the hell out of there.

The woman was the color of chalk and a pool of blood spread out from under her. It was no good. He could do nothing for her.

He burst through the double doors and into the dining area. His feet tangled up with one of the plump bodies littering the floor and slammed face to face into a dead man. Their teeth clicked and Juan screamed, but rolled away and jumped back to his feet.

The front of the restaurant was a shattered mess. He pumped his legs and ran toward it, feeling the fresh air of the night.

He stopped in his tracks when he heard the voice. A Chinese voice…singing?

It came from Mr. Chan's office.

Juan made a dash toward it. He stood in the doorway and could only stare. A CD player emitted the music, but that's not what caught his attention.

The bills fluttered in the wind blowing in from the broken windows. The safe's door stood open and piles of money lay in front of it.

Juan's mustache twitched so hard he sneezed. He ran into the office and kicked the safe door wider with the toe of his shoe. Jammed full of money.

Juan looked over his shoulder. The faint sound of a siren somewhere in the distance tickled his ear, and he quickened his pace.

It looked as if Mr. Chan was ready to make a run for it before his customers consumed him and his restaurant. A sack that looked big enough for Santa Claus lay beside the safe, piles of money already inside of it. Juan grabbed armfuls of cash and threw it into the bag. He moved as quickly as he could, keeping his ear sharp for that siren.

Sweat stung his eyes and salted his mouth. When he got the last of it in, he was about to slam the safe shut when a sheet of paper swung out and spiraled in the air before landing on his shoe.

Chinese symbols decorated the page, and he couldn't decipher any of it, but he had a feeling he knew what it was.

Juan grabbed the paper, stared at it for a second before tossing it in with the money. *I won't abuse it,* he thought. *I'll get this translated…and I'll do it right.*

KEEP EATING

Lola woke up on the floor, could barely move her head, let alone the rest of her body. She thought she was dead. The bright light of the fluorescent shining down from the ceiling sent pounding throbs through her brain.

The Mexican man was gone.

But she heard them. In the cooler. A large pile of kitchen debris had been shoved against the door. It blurred as she looked at it.

They gurgled and moaned and whimpered from inside. There was the unmistakable sound of chewing and tearing and slurping and smacking. They had their prize. What they'd wanted all along.

She wanted them to eat. Eat to their heart's desire. Until every scrap of food was gone, until the cooler was empty.

Blood seeped out from the bottom of the cooler door.

Finished already?

They would eat each other alive until there was nothing left. She smiled as she listened. The cries and snorts and growls as they devoured each other, themselves.

She listened for Daddy's voice. But he wasn't there.

Blue and red light flashed over the floor and walls and ceiling. She heard shouting and running footsteps.

"Keep eating…you b-bastards."

And the bright light became an endless darkness.

GRAND OPENING

Sebastian used his tortilla to sop up the rest of the sauce. The best goddamn meal he'd ever had. There was no question about that. He swiveled his head and looked at the new restaurant, a place he would be visiting again.

Manuel's.

He stood from the table, patted his stomach, left a hefty tip for the waitress. Claudia was her name. A damn pretty Mexican gal.

"Sir, you enjoy the food?" she said, shining that bright smile at him.

"Incredible. You guys will be seeing plenty of me, I can tell you that. My compliments to the chef."

She smiled. "My husband. Oh…here he is."

Sebastian followed Claudia's gaze toward the approaching man. A thick black mustache stood over his grin, twitched a couple of times.

The restaurant was full of smiling customers. They nodded as they chewed and widened their eyes with every bite.

"Another happy customer," Claudia said, then kissed her husband on the cheek.

"Yes, I'm very impressed."

The Mexican man shook Sebastian's outstretched hand. "Thank you, sir. Always my dream to own restaurant."

"Yes, he loves to cook."

"Well, I'm glad for it. You'll be seeing me, friend. Probably sooner than later."

As Sebastian made for the door, he stopped in his tracks. He turned to face the hugging couple. An older Mexican woman had joined them, her wrinkled fingers gripping the shoulders of a darling little girl.

"You know what…maybe I'll take a little something to go."

SHANE MCKENZIE is the author of *Infinity House* and *All You Can Eat*, but has multiple other projects from various publishers coming soon. He is also the editor at Sinister Grin Press. He lives in Austin, TX with his wife Melinda and daughter Maxine. You can keep up with him at his website www.shanemckenzie.org. Shane welcomes all emails from his readers: shane.p.mckenzie@gmail.com.

deadite
press

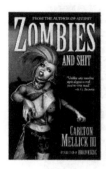

"Zombies and Shit" Carlton Mellick III - Twenty people wake to find themselves in a boarded-up building in the middle of the zombie wasteland. They soon discover they have been chosen as contestants on a popular reality show called Zombie Survival. Each contestant is given a backpack of supplies and a unique weapon. Their goal: be the first to make it through the zombie-plagued city to the pick-up zone alive. But because there's only one seat available on the helicopter, the contestants not only have to fight against the hordes of the living dead, they must also fight each other.

"Jack's Magic Beans" Brian Keene - It happens in a split-second. One moment, customers are happily shopping in the Save-A-Lot grocery store. The next instant, they are transformed into bloodthirsty psychotics, interested only in slaughtering one another and committing unimaginably atrocious and frenzied acts of violent depravity. Deadite Press is proud to bring one of Brian Keene's bleakest and most violent novellas back into print once more. This edition also includes four bonus short stories:

"Just Like Hell" Nate Southard- Dillion is a popular high school football star, gay, and tied to a chair in the dark. His lover is bound and gagged next to him. Around him are his teammates -- his captors. They aren't happy that they've been playing with a "faggot" and they intend to repay the disgrace. There will be humiliation, blood, and pain. But then it gets out of control. What started as black-hearted entertainment has turned into a cat-and-mouse game of gruesome justice. By the end of this night, four people will be dead. And those left alive will be forever scared.

"Depraved" Bryan Smith - Welcome to Hopkins Bend. You're never getting out of here alive... In the middle-of-nowhere, USA, there is a town not on any map. A place where outsiders are tortured, raped, and eaten. Where local law enforcement runs a sex trafficking ring. And the woods hold even more monstrous secrets. Today four unlucky travelers will end up in Hopkins Bend. If they want to ever get out alive they will have to become just as vicious and violent as their pursuers. Just as depraved.

Horror That'll Carve a Smile on Your Face.

CUT CORNERS VOLUME 1
Ramsey Campbell, Bentley Little, & Ray Garton

Peel your eyes open, get comfortable, and let three of the horror genre's hardest hitters take you for a ride. Prepare yourselves, my friends, for you are placing your sanity in the hands of these masters of the macabre.

Three brand new stories guaranteed to slice open a smile.

SACRIFICE
Wrath James White

All over town, little girls are going missing and turning up starved, dehydrated, and nearly catatonic. One man is eaten alive by his own dog along with half the pets in the neighborhood. An elementary school teacher is beaten to death by his own students while being stung by thousands of bees. It's up to Detective John Malloy and his partner Detective Mohammed Rafik to figure out how it's all connected to a mysterious voodoo priestess with the power to take away all of your hatred ... all of your fear ... all of your pain.

THE KILLINGS
J.F. Gonzalez & Wrath James White

In 1911, Atlanta's African American community was terrorized by a serial killer that preyed on young bi-racial women, cutting their throats and mutilating their corpses. In the 1980s, more than twenty African American boys were murdered throughout Atlanta. In 2011, another string of sadistic murders have begun, and this time it's more brutal than ever. If Carmen Mendoza, an investigative reporter working for Atlanta's oldest newspaper, can solve the murders, she may find the key to ending the violent curse gripping Atlanta's Black community. If not, she might just become the next victim.

WWW.SINISTERGRINPRESS.COM

Lightning Source UK Ltd.
Milton Keynes UK
UKHW010710160223
417123UK00005B/430

9 781621 050315